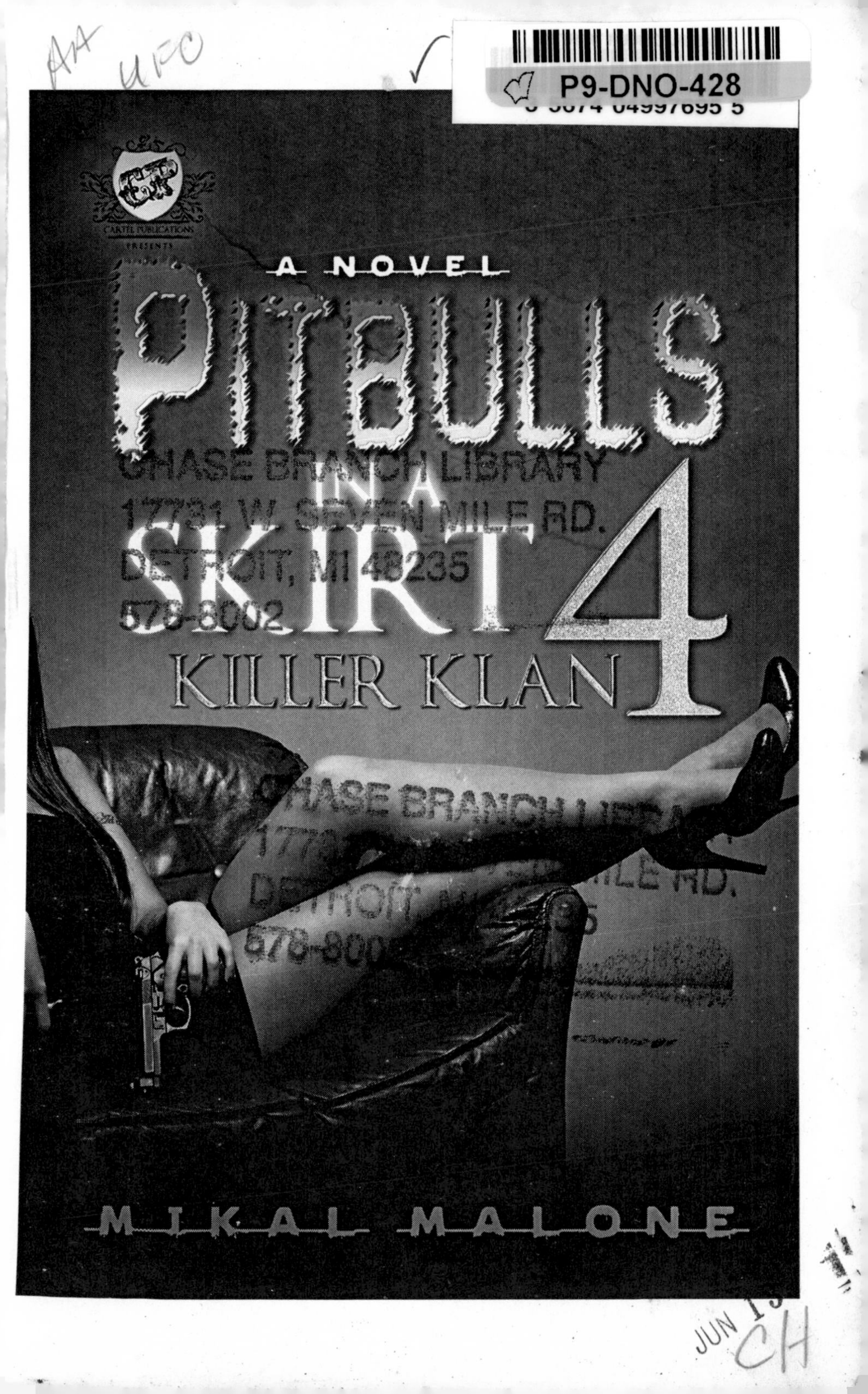
CARTEL PUBLICATIONS
PRESENTS
A NOVEL
PITBULLS
IN A
SKIRT 4
KILLER KLAN
MIKAL MALONE

PUBLISHER'S NOTE:
This book is a work of fiction. Names, characters, businesses, Organizations, places, events and incidents are the product of the Author's imagination or are used fictionally. Any resemblance of Actual persons, living or dead, events, or locales are entirely coincidental.

Library of Congress Control Number: 2013933521
ISBN 10: 098499307X
ISBN 13: 978-0984993079

Cover Design: Davida Baldwin www.oddballdsgn.com
Editor: Advanced Editorial Services
Graphics: Davida Baldwin
www.thecartelpublications.com
First Edition

Printed in the United States of America

CHECK OUT OTHER TITLES BY THE CARTEL PUBLICATIONS

FROM THE PUBLISHER'S DESK

What's Good Babies,

It's PBIAS time! Pitbulls In A Skirt 4 explodes with emotion, when the sins of the past come back for revenge. One thing we can be certain of is that you'll fall deeper in love with the ladies you've grown to adore, we guarantee it!

Keeping in line with Cartel tradition, we would like to honor a go-getter in life and business. In this letter, we would like to pay tribute to:

Davida Baldwin

Davida Baldwin is a trailblazer in the urban fiction industry and beyond. Not only has Davida, and her company Oddball Designs, spearheaded the graphic design for The Cartel Publications, Davida's work has been seen throughout the book world. Including but not limited to the book covers of New York Times best selling authors Ashley & Jaquavis, Wahida Clark and many more. Davida is the one-stop shop for graphic design as it pertains to book covers, websites, photography and so much more. We couldn't do it without Davida. We absolutely cherish her!

Ok, let me get back to work. Until we hug again.

T. Styles
President & CEO
The Cartel Publications
www.thecartelpublications.com
www.twitter.com/authortstyles
www.facebook.com/authortstyles

DEDICATION

I dedicate this to all Pitbulls In A Skirt Fans.
We are in a world of our own.

PROLOGUE

The moon acted as Mercedes' partner in crime, as it lit up the highway as she prepared to commit murder. The odometer read 90 miles as she straddled the yellow line up interstate 495, but still it wasn't fast enough. Too many cars were on the road, and they were holding her back, slowing her up from reaching her destination. So she made her own lane as she chased Karen, leader of the Killer Klan to save her flesh and blood.

"If this bitch hurt my grandbaby I'm gonna be on some serial killer type shit," Mercedes promised the world. She piloted the steering wheel right, and then left as if she were playing a video game and not with their lives.

"You gonna kill us instead," Carissa yelled at her from the passenger seat. She removed the black leather jacket she was wearing because suddenly she was too hot. "Slow down, Mercedes. Please."

"She's right," Yvette said from the backseat. Her short black hair was slicked back, because when she got the news that the baby was in danger, she didn't have time to style it. "If you don't be careful we'll never be able to get him back."

Mercedes ignored them as she pushed the limits of her custom painted gold E-Class. When her hands got too sweaty, she wiped them on the tight red jeans she was wearing, which was stained with the coffee she was drinking earlier. She dropped it on herself when she heard the news that Karen had taken the baby.

Mercedes eyes were fixed on the taillights of Karen's silver Range Rover, and she was determined not to let her out of her sight.

"Mercedes, please slow down," Carissa pled. It looked as if they were about to hit every car they approached and passed. "We can't do anything if you kill us. And if you think I don't care, let me remind you that your grandson is mine too."

"Shut the fuck up," Mercedes finally said, clipping the side of a black Nissan Sentra. The driver pulled over to the side of the road thinking Mercedes would follow him to exchange insurance information, but Mercedes kept it moving.

"Had I not listened to you," Mercedes continued, "and pushed off on that bitch when I wanted to I wouldn't be trying to save his life right now. All you give a fuck about is Persia's shiftless ass. You can't see nothing or nobody else. Not even your youngest daughter Treasure."

Carissa huffed and puffed after hearing Mercedes' statement. They were like sisters, and had been through everything together, but lately they failed at getting along.

PITBULLS IN A SKIRT 4

The anger Carissa felt in her heart at the moment didn't make her scared of a car accident anymore. She was suddenly emboldened. "You better watch how you talk to me, Mercedes. I have loved you for a long time, but I can become your enemy in a heartbeat."

Mercedes was done chit-chatting with her. When she saw the sign that read 'Woodrow Wilson Bridge' in the distance, her heart flapped wildly in her chest. She placed one hand over her breast, and maintained the steering wheel with the other.

"Where is she going, ya'll?" Mercedes was crying so hard it was difficult to see the road in front of her. "Where is she taking the baby?"

"I'm not sure," Yvette responded loading her .45 in the backseat. "But I do know this, the moment she parks that mothafucka I'm putting something hot in her brain. You just make sure you grab the baby when I do." She cocked her weapon to put one in the chamber.

When Mercedes followed her up the ramp on the bridge, she felt faint. "She's going to—,"

"Don't say that shit," Carissa yelled at her. "Don't say what's on your mind. I can hear what you thinking from over here, and Karen's not that crazy."

But, it was too late to guess what was about to happen, because Karen had already pulled on the side of the bridge, parked and ran toward the passenger door. She grabbed the baby out of the car seat, and stood on the side of the road. Cars passing her honked their horns wildly thinking she was about to jump into traffic.

It seemed like Mercedes couldn't get to the Range Rover fast enough. When she was finally a few feet away from Karen's truck, she decided to pull over and run the rest of the way. The front of her Benz slammed into the cement ramp, and their upper bodies were thrown forward, before being thrust roughly back into the black leather seats. Adrenaline was so high now that Carissa and Yvette jumped out of the car, as if nothing happened, despite the blood from the accident pouring over their bodies. Once out of the car they rushed toward Karen.

Mercedes, on the other hand, couldn't move from behind the wheel. She was watching her life flash before her eyes as Karen held onto the baby. When Mercedes saw Karen's mouth moving, she finally forced herself out of the car.

"Stay where you are," Karen yelled to be heard over the passing cars. "If you come any closer I'll throw this baby over the edge."

"Karen," Mercedes yelled, "please don't do whatever you're thinking about doing. I'm begging you."

"Then you better stay the fuck back. All of you," Karen told the three of them. "I'm more serious now then I've ever been in my entire life."

The three of them didn't move any closer.

"I'll stay back here," Yvette advised. "But if you hurt that baby I'm blowing your ribs out," she threatened. "Do you hear what I'm saying?"

"You think I give a fuck about dying?" Karen replied. "Black Water, thy father, is waiting on me in Heaven. He has assured me before he died that if I live my life according to his word, that I will be okay. So there's nothing you can do to threaten me."

"Well what do you want," Mercedes questioned. "Because whatever you want I can give it to you. I'm a very wealthy woman, Karen. And, I can give you anything your heart desires. Just speak on it."

Karen laughed. "It's just like you bitches to think everything is about money. What I want runs deeper than monetary value."

"I'll give you whatever you're asking," Mercedes said. "Just say the word."

"I want salvation," her wild eyes looked into Mercedes'. "Can you give me salvation for abandoning one of my commandments? If you can't, this baby can give me salvation with his life."

Mercedes paused a few moments to consider the question. She knew that Karen, and the rest of the Black Water Klan members, were brainwashed into believing Black Water's fake doctrine. Black Water had mind-fucked the Klan so long that they believed everything he said. So if Mercedes wanted to get through to her, she had to think smartly.

"Karen, I don't know what you mean by salvation," Mercedes started. "But, I will give you my life

if you don't hurt my baby. Please. My life for the child."

Karen looked into Mercedes' eyes, smiled, and jumped off of the Woodrow Wilson Bridge, with the baby in her arms.

CHAPTER 1

MERCEDES

PRESENT DAY

I'm sitting in the passenger's seat of Yvette's Bentley, texting Derrick from my iPhone. We are back together, but things feel different. I still can't get over him fucking the girl Bucky behind my back, and I don't know if I ever will. I haven't even told my friends that we're back together, because I know they won't want to hear it. As far as they are concerned Derrick is disloyal, and he should be banished from my life. I know that they are right, but what about my heart? What about my vows to stand with him through sickness and in health?

'Were are you D? I miss you. Hit me back.'

I throw the phone in my lap, and turn up the air conditioner. The cool breeze blows against my face, and causes my long black hair to fly back into the leather seat.

When I look at the buildings someone told us belonged to the Black Water Klan, I frown. I'm so tired of dealing with these sick mothafuckas. I want my life back, and I want this shit behind me. *Behind us.*

Carissa, Yvette and my friend Toi are with me, and we are scoping the scene so that we can come back later and finish off the rest of the Klan. I want these mothafuckas dead. For years they have been tormenting my family and me. They even killed Kenyetta, one of my best friends. And, they also tried to kill my son, and me.

Our first involvement with them came when Cameron, my first love, decided to team up with Black Water to take back Emerald City when me and my girls took it from him and his boys. Of course the shit backfired in Cameron's face when my girls and me maintained what we built, and I killed Cameron.

The second involvement came when Kenyetta, my good friend, started fucking with Black Water, because she didn't realize he ran Tyland Towers, a rival project and drug operation near Emerald City. But he knew exactly who she was and what he was doing. Although Lil C runs Tyland now, and re-named it Camelot, back in those days Emerald City and Tyland Towers had major beef. But just like every time somebody tries to cross us, we killed Black Water too, and maintained control of Emerald City.

Our final involvement with the Klan came when Tamir, Black Water's son, tried to kill Lil C and us to seek revenge. It happened when I was over cousin Vickie's house, and Carissa showed up unannounced. I didn't feel like dealing with her at the time, because Yvette and me were fighting an assault charge from my husband's sidepiece, Bucky. So, my mind was not in the right place to be talking to Carissa.

Carissa was talking to me about Persia going missing and how Lil C fucked her, and got her pregnant. Anyway while we were outside of Vickie's house, somebody started shooting at us. I thought Lil C was trying to kill me at first when I looked down the street and saw his angry face. Besides, he learned that I killed his father Cameron, and still held some resentment. But it turned out that he was firing at Tamir who was also at Vickie's house, waiting to kill me. Lil C murdered him and we put that part of the Black Water Klan behind us. But now, it's time to get rid of the entire family. I have no doubt that the longer we allow them to live, the higher the chances are of them trying us again.

"Where the fuck is everybody?" Toi says looking at the buildings. "We been out here for twenty minutes and not one soul has walked out."

"I don't know, but this is definitely the address." I respond looking at the piece of paper in my lap.

"Maybe they're inside fucking each other," Carissa laughs to herself.

The Black Water Klan was known for incest, so I know where she was going with that statement.

"Oh shit," Yvette yells looking out of the window. "Is that Persia?" She points.

We all focus on one of the buildings again. And, there that bitch Persia was, walking out of the building with some woman. Persia's stomach was a little big, and it was evident that she was pregnant. Supposedly it's Lil C's child but I don't believe it. And if you ask me do I fuck with Persia I gotta say no. It was because of her, that Lil C knew I killed his father. And it was because of my no-good-ass friend Carissa in the back seat, that Persia even knew that much. Why Carissa would discuss what we do in the streets to her child is beyond me.

Anyway, Persia used the secret she learned about me killing Cameron to try to win Lil C back. But, he didn't fuck with her now, and he probably won't fuck with her in the future.

"Yeah...but what the fuck is she doing here?" Yvette says looking out of the window at Persia. "I didn't even know that she knew them." She turns the air off and rolls down the window.

"Oh my God," Carissa says covering her mouth with both hands. "That's my baby and she's still pregnant!"

"Right...but with whose baby?" I say.

"Don't fucking start with me! You know whose baby she's carrying." Carissa replies. "Your grandchild at that."

She can believe that shit if she wants to, but I don't.

"If it's true," Yvette says interrupting us. "C not gonna want her anywhere near these fuckers."

"Fuck this, I'm going out there," Carissa responds opening her car door. She jumps out and rushes toward Persia. She is so focused on her daughter that she was almost hit by a silver Yukon.

"Watch where the fuck you're going!" the driver yells at Carissa before pulling off.

"Fuck you!" Yvette says from the car, smashing the horn in Carissa's defense.

"Baby, what are you doing here?" Carissa yells at Persia looking her over.

"Ma?" Persia's eyes widen. "How did you find me?" She places her hand over her eyes to shield the sun.

"Don't worry about that, you're still my daughter and you're coming with me," Carissa yells trying to grab her hand. Persia backs away and hides behind the woman's back.

"I can't," Persia says looking at the woman, "this is my family now."

"Fuck that…I want to take care of you, and your baby, honey," Carissa persists. "I'm sorry about everything we've gone through, please come home."

"I'm not going anywhere," Persia persists balling up her fists. From where I'm sitting it looks as if she wants to hit Carissa. "Leave me alone!"

Carissa is better than me, because if I wanted Persia's ass to come home, I would've snatched her by her hair by now.

When more people come out of the building, and flood the streets, I know things are way too serious.

"Let's go break this shit up." Yvette says to us.

Yvette didn't have to tell me though, because Toi and me jump out of the car and join the crowd. I have my nine tucked under my pink-t-shirt, and I know Yvette and Toi are strapped too. No, I didn't want to fight for this little girl, because I don't like her, but I'll go down shooting for my girls.

"Fuck are ya'll doing here?" one of the men says to us. "She doesn't belong to you anymore."

"What kind of sick shit is this?" I ask ready to put something hot in his skull if he moves to quickly or closely. "You can't just take a child and think shit is sweet. She is a fucking minor!"

"We can take better care of her than her own mother can," says a woman.

Carissa looks crushed when she says that. "I don't know what the fuck is going on, but I am not leaving here without my daughter!" Carissa cries. The crowd is so thick now no one can drive on the street, without hitting us.

"Where's Cheese?" someone yells into the crowd.

"He's not here!" says someone else.

"Somebody go get Karen," another screams. "Tell her we got outsiders out here!"

"Yeah, get Karen, bitch," Yvette yells at him. "Like we give a fuck!"

"Karen must be their fake ass leader." I say to my girls. "Ya'll packing right?"

Toi and Yvette place their hands in their purses. Yvette says, "You already know it." I hear the soft cock of her gun.

And then we waited. Waited for the person they call Karen to appear. As I linger, I look at the strange black faces amongst the crowd. We share the same heritage, and probably speak the same language, but I can tell they don't understand me, or recognize me. Their eyes look closed off to me, and the outside world. It's hard to describe, but their faces remind me of one of Yvette's Pitbulls. It can't speak, but it seems like it wants so hard to understand, but most of all, it wants to kill. I can only imagine what sick things Black Water has pushed into their minds when he was alive.

A few minutes later, I hear a female's voice ring out through the crowd. Maybe it's Karen, but I can't see her face.

"What's going on?" she says.

"We got trouble over there!" another person answers as the crowd parts from the entrance of the building.

Finally I see her face. The one I believe is Karen is extraordinarily beautiful, and I am surprised because I was expecting a monster. She is about 5'4, and appears to be about thirty-something. A small mole rests on the tip of her nose and her honey brown face is flawless. Her hair is dirty brown, but her eyes are hazel. She's carrying a red leather book, which resembles a bible, in her hands. Although she is extremely attractive, I'm not dumb enough to assume she's harmless, by letting my guards down. I mean look at my friends and me. We could work the pages of any Victoria Secret magazine, but we could blow your face off too.

Karen walks next to Persia, and the woman. The crowd behind her closes, as if they are locking a back door. I've been in a lot of dangerous situations before in my lifetime, but this takes the cake. They look like trained killers, ranging from pre-teen all the way up to adults.

At first Karen is frowning until she looks at Yvette. Carissa and I stand next to Yvette, and Toi stands behind Yvette. If this person they call Karen gets wild, I will take her life, no questions asked, before they take mine.

Yvette steps up to Karen. Her eyes look soft, and not as angry as before. "Cecil?" Yvette says covering her mouth.

Karen's eyebrows rise and her head tilts slightly to the right. She leans in and says, "Oh my, God! Yvette…is that you?"

This is odd to me because I know everybody my friends know. There isn't a person alive who they have hung with, that I have never met before. Still, I don't know this person. Who is she? And what does she want with my best friend?

"What's going on?" I ask Yvette.

Yvette doesn't answer me. Instead I notice Yvette's shoulders don't seem as stiff anymore. She looks like a kid, instead of the crime-killer-boss I know her to be.

"Who is this, Yvette?" I ask her.

Yvette still doesn't say shit to me, and I'm irritated. I need to know if this is a friend or foe. Instead of putting me at ease or on guard, Yvette reaches out for Cecil/Karen and pulls her into her arms. Karen embraces her.

The mob behind Cecil/Karen seems to be as confused as I am. When they move closer, I bust three shots in the air. The first two are a warning, but the last shot could've hit the bitch who been mean mugging me from the moment I walked over here, if I lowered my gun just a little.

"If anybody walks up on her it's gonna be a fucking problem," I tell them all. Carissa and Toi aim their weapons into the crowd along with me. "So, make a move if that's how you feeling."

Cecil/Karen separates from Yvette and says, "There's no need for violence." She turns around to her people who had yet to give us the breathing room that we desired. They were so close to us that I could smell their breaths. "Everything is fine," Cecil/Karen says to them, "back up a little."

A young attractive man with light brown hair, wearing navy blue eyeglasses struts up to Cecil/Karen. "Ma, who are these people?"

He looks like the kind of boy Persia would be into, older in his mannerisms, but young in the face. He puts me in the mind of a young Malcolm X. He had some kind of authority with the Klan, I can tell by how his eyes never leave mine, and his shoulders stand high. He wants me to know that he's not afraid. Little does he know, not being afraid of us makes him stupid, not smart.

"Oscar, go back inside, and take the family with you," Cecil/Karen says to him.

Oscar doesn't budge. He looks at her and says, "But, ma—,"

"Son, go," she yells pointing toward the building. The crowd opens up to allow him room to walk back, but still he doesn't move. "Now," Cecil/Karen says more firmly.

"If you wish," he says with an attitude before looking at me evilly. "Family, let's go inside," he yells to the crowd. Before walking into the building he focuses on two other teenagers by the door. "Roman and Lance, you stay out here, and protect Ma and Persia with your lives."

"We on it," the younger one responds.

When the crowd dispersed I got a good look at Roman and Lance. I don't know why, but for some reason their names and faces are familiar to me. But we ran into so many of their members that I couldn't be sure. The one, who moved to the name Roman, was young, about eight years old if I had to pick a number. The other was probably in his late teens.

Eventually the crowd, following Oscar, disappears into the building.

"Where have you been?" Yvette says to Karen/Cecil, with tears rolling down her face. "I haven't seen you in forever. I can't even believe I'm standing in front of you right now."

"I've had a hard life," Cecil/Karen replies. "A real hard life."

"Can somebody tell us what's going on?" Carissa asks Yvette, although her eyes remain on her pregnant-freaked out-daughter.

"I'm sorry, ya'll," Yvette says turning around to look at us. "She's cool. This is my oldest sister, Cecil." Yvette looks at me. "You remember right, Mercedes? She's the one I told you about that my mother abandoned."

My jaw drops. Years ago I remember Yvette mentioning her sister, but I put it out of my mind, because she didn't bring it up to me again. It may have hurt too much that she had a sister in the world, but not a relationship. Truthfully before we had to kill her mother some months back, for trying to set us up, I thought we were the only family Yvette had. In my opinion we're the only family any of us need. I don't trust this person named Cecil. I don't trust her sister.

"Wow, I forgot you had a sister," Carissa says. She extends her hand to Cecil/Karen. Cecil/Karen shakes it with a smile. "I feel better already about this situation."

Sometimes Carissa is extra green. I mean just because this chick is Yvette's sister doesn't mean she's cool, or won't do us harm. Blood don't mean shit these days unless it's in your own body. Remembering how we had to kill Yvette's mother for setting us up should remind Carissa of that fact. But as always she only sees what she wants to see.

"Can somebody explain to me what's going on?" Cecil/Karen says to us. "Are you kin to this child?"

"Yes, I'm her mother," Carissa replies.

"She said her mother died," Cecil/Karen says with a frown. "I'm confused."

"Cecil, I don't know what's going on here, but let me clear some things up," Yvette says softly. "Persia is a minor, and her mother is one of my best friends. This is her parent right here," she touches Carissa on the shoulder, "and she's been looking all over for her. We just happened to be out, and saw her here."

"Is that what brought you here?" Cecil/Karen says. "Did you show up because you knew she was with us?"

"I'm gonna be real with you," Yvette starts, "we got beef with the Black Water Klan. They took a lot of good people from us. But, all of that shit went out of the window when we saw Persia, and I saw you."

"Wait, you are a part of the Emerald City squad?"

"I am," Yvette confirms with a nod of the head.

"I didn't know. I never saw you before."

"It doesn't matter," Yvette says. "All that matters now is this. I want to be diplomatic about this shit so Persia can get back with her family. I'm done with the war, Cecil. My girls are too."

"My mother don't give a fuck about me," Persia says rolling her eyes at Yvette.

"Persia, slow your roll," Yvette warns. "I'm talking amongst adults. If I want your opinion on a matter best believe you'll know."

"Don't be so mean to her, Yvette," Carissa responds. "She's pregnant."

"So because she's pregnant that means she gets to fly off at the lips?" Yvette questions. "Naw, Car, you know I don't play that shit. A child stays in a child's place even if I gotta put her there."

"Listen, someone close to the family brought her to us some time back," Cecil/Karen responds. "She said a lot of things about her family life, and it made us concerned which is why we didn't call the police. We were afraid to return her to her violent past. But, I am more than willing to work this out with you Carissa, if it'll be for the benefit of us all."

"It will be for the benefit," Carissa responds.

"Good," Yvette smiles again. "That works for us." Yvette hugs Cecil/Karen again. "I'm sure we can come up with something fair."

I'm confused though. What did we just decide? Is this fresh little bitch coming back with us or not?

"I'm so glad I found you," Yvette says to her sister. "There's so much that has happened. I gotta tell you about ma, and the shit she pulled some months back. Cecil, I swear you won't believe this shit when you hear it. Ma actually was about to set me up on some wild shit. Luckily me and my girls were on it."

Suddenly the mood changes. Cecil/Karen pushes Yvette backwards and I instinctively place my gun against the pulse of her temple. Carissa and Toi follow my lead by lining up their barrels to her head too. We weren't the only ones preparing for a gun battle, because Roman and Lance ran up to us and pulled out their weapons. Somebody was going to die. The question was who?

"What's going on?" I ask Yvette although I'm looking at Cecil/Karen. "I thought you said this chick was cool."

"She is," Yvette says softly. She doesn't sound sure though. Why isn't she sure? "Cecil—,"

"Karen," she interrupts. "I go by Karen now." Her eyes are now pulled closely together and she's frowning.

Persia, on the other hand, is grinning so widely I felt like knocking her in the face with the butt of my gun. I would've done it, but I didn't feel like dealing with Carissa afterwards. She sensitive about that type of thing. All of this shit is Persia's fault anyway.

"Did I just do something?" Yvette asks Karen. "I mean one minute we were bonding and the next you pushing me away."

"You know what, Yvette, for the longest time I hated you," Karen says. "I know it wasn't your fault, but I couldn't get the feeling out of my heart that ma chose you, instead of me."

"Karen, don't put that shit on me," Yvette says. "That wasn't my fault. I was a kid, and I thought about you everyday of my life."

"It probably wasn't your fault, but at the end of the day, ma made a decision that she could take care of you, but not me." Tears roll down her face. "And, now I hear you're still in contact with her?" She yells. "But what about me? Who cared that I was sold to a white dry-cleaning storeowner for fifty bucks? Who, when he was finished with me, gave me to his friend after losing in a Poker game? My life was taken from me, and yet she stayed by your side. That's all I ever wanted, for my mother to love me. But she never did. I never experienced real love until now, with my new family."

"Karen, I'm sorry," Yvette says holding a hand over her chest. "But you can't put that beef on me. That was ma. I never forgave her for abandoning you either. And I didn't trust her—,"

"Save the shit, 'Vette," Karen says with a wave of her hand.

"Save the shit?" Yvette repeats.

"Exactly, but let me make this clear too," Karen exhales, "I will honor what I said to you all earlier, about facilitating the meeting with Persia, and her mother." She clutches her red book tighter. "But, I will not turn her over until I'm sure she will be safe. Unlike what Ma did to me, the Black Water Klan takes care of their own. But, my involvement in your family's life is going to cost you."

"So she's a member of the Black Water Klan now?" I ask, gun still trained to Karen's head. As a matter of fact, everyone was still aimed but Yvette, Karen and Persia.

"Yes," Karen says flatly. "And, we won't release her until we're ready." She snaps her fingers, and

Lance and Roman lower their weapons and walk Persia toward the building. "I'll be in contact with you all regarding my fee," Karen continues. "I'm sure Persia knows how to reach you."

"Baby, don't leave," Carissa screams at Persia. She runs toward her before Toi lowers her weapon, and pulls Carissa back toward us.

"Don't do it like this," Toi tells Carissa. "Let her go for now. We know where she at."

Carissa shakes away from Toi. "How do you know I just won't call the police?" she yells at Karen. "You got my daughter. She's a fucking minor."

"Because you and I both know you'll never see her again," Karen says seriously. "I'll assist in helping her get away, and I have many resources at my disposal. Trust me when I say I can make her a ghost if I choose."

"You wrong for this shit," Yvette says.

Karen looks back at Yvette. "I don't ever want to see you around here again. Do you hear what I'm saying, Yvette?"

Yvette remains silent.

"Then it's settled," Karen continues.

"What's to stop me from killing you right now?" I ask Karen. "It ain't like your people out here anymore. If we wanted, we could kill you, run up in that bitch and bring Persia out ourselves."

Karen nods up at the building on the left and right. Every window was open, and every window had a barrel pointed in our direction. Her men were on guard like the soldiers in Emerald City. We are clearly outnumbered.

"Don't be dumb," Karen smirks. "Be smart and live."

"You know this is not over," I say.

"It never is."

CHAPTER 2
YVETTE
(THREE MONTHS LATER)

The sun turns my silver Bentley into liquid platinum, as I cruise down the highway. I like my ride, but truth be told I'm a truck-kind-of girl, and I can't wait to get the new red Range Rover I had been coveting.

I open a vanilla scented tree air freshener, and hang it on my rearview mirror. I'm on my way to deliver Lil C his package. I could've given this job to one of my soldiers in Emerald City, since we own it again, but I don't trust anybody handing off work to my nephew, whether he's a drug boss or not.

The cell phone lying in my lap is warm, because I called my ex-girlfriend Chris so many times trying to reach her that I guess my battery was heating up. I can't believe that almost a year ago, we lived together in my townhouse in Georgetown, a suburb of Washington DC.

So much has changed since then. Starting with the fact that Bucky, the bitch Derrick was fucking behind Mercedes' back, called the police on me,

Mercedes and Toi, after we jumped her in the laundry room. I was arrested for that shit some time after that. How scandalous. She totally disregarded the code, no snitching or calling the cops…ever.

When I made it to jail to answer for the beat down, I saw Chris who was also inside for some speeding tickets she failed to pay. The crazy part is, she acted like she didn't know me when I approached her. Chris' exact words were, *'Do I know you?'*

I'm telling you I could've killed her, but my heart had too much love inside of it for her at the time to take her life. Plus, I was the reason we weren't together anymore, because all Chris wanted to do was to love me. She practically begged me to give our relationship a chance, but I rejected her. I wasn't sure about the gay lifestyle, and I'm still not.

The next thing I know, I came home one day and her clothes were gone. She moved out, and I haven't been the same since.

When Mercedes bailed me out of jail, I waited for a while before reaching out to Chris. At first she was giving me a hard time by not accepting my calls, but eventually she gave in. The thing is, the nature of our relationship had shifted. It was no longer about us; it was all about sex.

I wasn't tripping too hard because I had been spending time with Judah, our new drug connect. But, Judah was just a thing; he wasn't where my heart lied and I'm not sure if he would ever be. I guess I was still in love with Chris, but how do you give your heart so freely, when it's been broken before?

I don't like being in love, although I can't live without it. I don't like my mood being impacted by a person leaving me, not calling me, or hurting my feelings. I can't run a business like that, and I can't function with someone in my head. After Thick played games with my heart and mind, I can't see opening up so easily, although for some reason, for Chris anyway, I want to.

Last week shit changed again for Chris and me when I found out that although I was only fucking Judah on the side, Chris had actually fallen for a bank teller name Lace.

If we wanted to see each other we had to sneak behind Lace's back. But I'm sick of living like that. I'm use to having what I want these days, and I don't want that to change. Today I was planning to tell Chris that if she wanted to be with me, she would have to leave Lace alone. The only thing is I'm not sure if she will choose me. And, if she does am I ready to do right by her? I guess I'll cross the last bridge when I get there.

When my phone rings I quickly answer it hoping its Chris.

"Hello."

"What up, Vette? How you holding up?"

I sigh. "Hey, Mercedes, what's up?"

"I asked you first. How are you holding up?" She repeats. "With this Karen thing and all?"

"Look, I told you I was going to wipe my hands of her and I stand behind my word."

"But you seemed so happy to see her."

"I was," I say. "But I can't force her to want a relationship with me. She acts like living with my mother was the American dream. That bitch was high and on drugs every day I lived with her, 'Cedes. So if that's how Karen or Cecil, or whatever the fuck she wants to be called, wants to carry shit, it'll be my pleasure to stay out of her life. I got too much shit going on anyway. If we are meant to be family, we will."

"So you came to the conclusion when?" she asks me. "Because just the other day you said you would do everything you could to reconnect with your sister."

"And I have, 'Cedes. And now I'm done," I roll down the window to let the cool breeze inside of my car. "Relax, I'm still the same gangster you fell in love with."

"That's good to hear because I was scared at first. So where are you about to go? To meet C?"

"Bye, Mercedes," I say hanging up on her.

I'm tired of playing the telephone man for Mercedes. I mean I know she wants a relationship with her son, but sometimes I feel like Carissa and her are obsessed with their children. Days like this make me grateful that I didn't have any children of my own. My soldiers are the only kids I need. They keep me plenty busy.

I shake my head and pull up to the driveway leading into Emerald City. The gates immediately open when the gatekeeper sees my face. I park in the field, grab my red Hermes bag and ease out of the car. I wave at all of my men in position in the yard and on the roofs. I smile when I catch the stare of my soldiers looking at my body. It's not their fault. They aren't trying to be disrespectful. This tight black pencil skirt I'm wearing is hugging my thick ass. I know it is because I picked it thinking I was hooking up with Chris later. And the weather is just like I love it. Not too hot, and not too cold.

Coming here reminds me about how we murdered Dreyfus in his own house. I always knew Emerald City would be mine again when he tried to take it from us, and I was right too.

I strut into the community center, and Lil C is already waiting on me inside. You can say one thing for him; he's always punctual.

Lil C is still so handsome. His brown skin seems to radiate and his curly hair is tamed into a low cut. A platinum chain, with the word Camelot dressed in Diamonds, lay against his black t-shirt. Five of his men are flanked on his sides, and they all give me my respect by way of salute, when I walk through the door.

Lil C stands up to greet me and we embrace. He doesn't sit down until I sit first. He has manners, even if he forgets them some times when it comes to his mother.

I open my Hermes purse; grab his package wrapped in black plastic. "That's all you," I tell him sliding the bag across the table.

One of his men walks toward me, brings me my money, and takes the package back to C. I don't bother counting his money. Lil C is always on point with the cash plus it ain't about that with us. He's family.

He eyeballs the package quickly and hands it back to his man. "Thanks, auntie. We doing good in Camelot so I'm going to have to up my work soon."

"You're welcome," I say. "And when you're ready I got you."

I contemplate putting in another word for Mercedes, even though I think it's a bad idea. I don't like my money convos to mix with family convos. But since he's ignoring her, I feel obligated. Mercedes is like a sister to me, and I want this shit between them done.

C is about to stand up to leave until I say, "When are you going to call your mother? It's time to make good with her."

Lil C flops back in the seat and rubs his hand over his curly hair. "Auntie, I thought we said we'll never discuss family over business."

"Far as I can see business is concluded," I say nodding at the package his man is holding. "Now give me the respect I deserve, and answer my question. Why aren't you connecting with your mother anymore, C? This shit is torturing her."

He sighs. "Because she killed my father," he says plainly. "And I won't forgive her for that. Ever. She deserves torture, and more."

"Lil C, she didn't kill him without merit," I say looking into his eyes. "You know first hand how much she loved that man. But he was vile, son. So he had to go. In the end it was her or him, and he lost."

"Don't talk about my fucking father like that," he yells.

I bite my tongue. I want to hurt him, but I try to connect with his pain. It's hard, if I'm being honest, to understand what the big deal is about Cameron. I didn't have a father in my corner or a mother. So I can't understand how it must feel to lose someone who was in your life since birth.

"C, your father wanted to murder your mother. And he was going to do it because she had moved on, and maintained control of Emerald City at the same time. Killing Cameron was the last resort. Trust me. She battled with his death because she knew her children needed him. I know this for a fact, C."

"Why did she lie to me?"

"Because there were some things nobody could put you on to, because you were a child. Truth be told, you still are."

"I'm eighteen now," he says. "And I might be young but I got major responsibility." He lifts the medallion off of his shirt, and releases it. It makes a small thud sound against his muscles. "If you ask me, I'm doing a good job too."

"You right about that," I nod in agreement. "Since you took over Tyland-,"

"Camelot," he says correcting me.

I chuckle. He's still the same punk kid to me, despite his height and his bigger dick size. "You got that. Since you took over Camelot things have been smooth. But, did you ever stop to think that the props you're getting may also be because of our rep? Mothafuckas know not to fuck with us, C. And you know why? Because we laid the murder game down early on, and we continue to do so."

"And I'm an adult."

"What?"

"You called me a child earlier, but I'm an adult now."

"Lil C, you are still a child," I say plainly banging my diamond-covered fist on the table. "And, you owe it to your mother to hear her out. Call her. Please. You only get one mother in life."

Lil C stands up, walks toward me and kisses me on the cheek. "I love you, Aunt Yvette. But, I'm a man now, and ya'll can't tell me what to do anymore. Since I was a kid I was raised in the drug game. When I should've been playing with toy cars with my friends, I was listening at the door to you, ma and the rest of my aunts talk shop. But nobody would ever bring me in but dad. Now he's gone, and I want to live out his legacy. I want to do him proud.

You gotta let me perfect my life, even if it's without my mother."

I see the look in his eyes. He's changed now. And, its only then that I understand that Mercedes may have lost him for good.

◄·································►

"Chris, I'm not trying to give you an ultimatum," I say to her while driving home from my meeting with Lil C. "But I don't understand why you think it's cool to fuck me, and leave me. You act like we didn't have a history."

"'Vette, I wanted the relationship. Do you recall?" She says reminding me of shit I wanted to forget. "And, you decided you didn't want to be with me anymore. So I moved on."

I'm gripping the steering wheel so tightly now my knuckles crack. When a tractor-trailer almost hits my car, probably because the driver didn't see me, I remember that I seriously can't wait to get my truck. I bonk my horn and pull back in front of the driver. Fuck him! I step on my brakes and right before he's about to hit me, I speed off. I can see the smoke from his wheels in my rearview mirror.

"Chris, we have a past," I say to her, focusing back on the call. "And I want to see if we can try again. Maybe we can get it right this time."

"Sorry, babes," she says. "But it's much too late for all that."

I'm embarrassed and broken. My heart is beating in my chest and I feel like a fool for throwing myself out there, only to be rejected. I guess her telling me that its too late doesn't hurt enough because I ask, "Do you love her?"

Without hesitation she says, "I do. Which is why I'm glad you brought this up. I was going to tell you that I can't see you no more, 'Vette. It's legal for women to marry now in DC, and I asked her to marry me. She said yes."

My chest tightens and I'm trying to breathe. There is no worst pain than losing the love of the one person who has always loved you. "Chris, please don't do this to me. It's okay for you to fuck this girl, but you getting too serious now. Don't let her take you from me."

"Naw, you did that yourself," Chris says. "I'ma always love you though. Bye."

I'm so mad I roll my window down and throw my iPhone onto the street. Tears wash over my cheekbones and my stomach swirls. I can't deal with this kind of pain. I just wanna get away for a few days, to get my mind right. Maybe I'll catch a flight to Cancun, Mexico. Yeah that's what I'll do.

I'm sobbing until I pull up in front of my townhouse, and see a red Range Rover parked out front with a white bow on the top. What the fuck? I park my car, hop out and remove the gun from my purse. I don't know if this is a set up, but if it is, I'll put so many holes in this mothafucka it will be totaled when I get through with it.

Slowly I approach the truck, gun aimed. When I get to the driver's side window, I see a letter on the seat with my name on it. I look around to be sure I'm not being cornered again. When everything looks safe, I open the door, and look in the back. The truck is empty. So I climb inside and read the letter.

'Vette, since I know you don't accept gifts, this one is going to cost you. Meet me at Sex Under The Sea. You know, the new restaurant surrounded by water. –Your Prince Judah'

I can't help but smile when I finish reading the letter, and look around my new ride. I can't believe Judah actually bought me the red Range I wanted. Sure I could buy an entire fleet of these in all colors with the money I have if I so desired. But, it was the thought that counted. Suddenly I realize something. Who needs a dom when you can fuck with a real nigga instead?

When I make it to the restaurant, I'm lead in by a pretty hostess with red hair, and pale cheeks. I feel like I'm in an ocean, and the scene is breathtaking. The walls, the floors, and even the ceilings are glass filled with water. Beautiful fish swim everywhere around us, and this is so romantic. I think Judah has outdone himself, until I see the bed in the middle of the restaurant. Next to it is a table and two chairs. They're the only table and chairs inside here. He must've bought out the entire restaurant for the day. That's the kind of thing you can do when you are a millionaire.

Judah approaches me in an all black everything suit. I can smell the Chanel men's cologne on his skin, and I melt. He hugs me tightly and rocks me in his arms. Damn, this man moves me sexually. I just wish I could love him, the way that he wants me too. Finally he pulls away from me and I run my hand over his yellow skin. He is still the finest man I've ever seen in my life. Thick couldn't touch him if he tried.

I know it's wrong to mix business with pleasure, and normally I wouldn't. I mean fucking with Judah even though he is our drug connect could backfire. But, it's been a long time since I've been in the company of a man, but more than anything, in the company of somebody who wanted me for me. Chris has made it clear that she doesn't want the relationship, so I'm going to try and live with her decision. May her and her new girlfriend live in rainbow heaven for the rest of their gay ass lives. I'm done with her.

"Where did you get this black dress from? You look so sexy." He runs his hand on the back of my short spiky haircut.

"If you like this, you should see what I'm wearing under it."

He winks. "Well let's hurry up and eat and get this show on the road," he responds.

He walks me over to the table, pulls out my chair. I sit, and then he takes a seat. The waiter brings out appetizers of shrimp cocktail, and follows it up with dinner salads. For the entrée he brought out broiled crab cakes, garlic mash potatoes and steamed asparagus. Everything was delicious but I knew something was up. You don't pull an event like this unless it's important.

When the waiter brings out the Crème Brule' I say, "Judah, what's up with all of this?"

"You don't like it?"

"I love it, but I want you to keep it real with me too."

He wipes his hands with the black cloth napkin and throws it on the table. "How you know me so well, when we only been kicking it for about six months?"

"Because, we spend a lot of time together," I admit. "Outside of my best friends, you're the only person I see more than four times a week. You learn a lot about a person when you remain quiet and listen to them. So tell me what's up?"

"You're right," he says, "and I only have people around me I care about."

"Judah, you're scaring me."

"Don't be scared".

He opens a bottle of Pinot Grigio and we drink glass after glass in complete silence. The next thing I know I'm buzzed, and on the bed while he's removing my dress. When my dress falls on the glass floor, he removes my silk pink La Perla bra and panty set.

Once I'm naked he lies on top of me. I open my legs so he can enter my box, but he doesn't go there right away. His warm body feels like a heated blanket against my skin, and I love the feeling. I run my hand over his bicep, before scaling my fingers along the muscles of his back.

"Yvette, you're so beautiful," he tells me. "Did I ever tell you that?"

Compliments are still hard for me to hear at times. When I was with Thick, he made me feel fat, dirty and worthless. So to hear complements from Judah, and even Chris when we were together, made me feel undeserving. Like they aren't being real with me. And, more than money I need people to be real with me. I guess I would feel more at home if they disrespected me, and made me feel inferior. At least I know where they're coming from then. I'm damaged in that way I guess.

"You tell me that every time I see you," I admit. Since I'm buzzing the water is making me feel like I'm on a boat. I hope I don't throw up.

"But, do you believe me?"

I don't believe him, but I don't want him to know it either. "Yes. I—,"

His hard dick entering my pussy interrupts my statement. He pushes into me slowly at first, until I'm filled up with him. His hairy stomach rubs against my belly. Judah kisses me on the side of my neck, and rocks his waist back and forth. I'm trembling and I lower my head, to nibble on his right shoulder. His light skin immediately reddens and I love it. If I'm being honest I'll say I'm probably marking my territory. If he is mine I want other bitches to know I've been here. I'm a control freak of sorts.

"Judah, you feel so good," I say pulling him toward me.

"You feel good too, mami," he says before sucking my right nipple softly. "I love you."

I don't know where it came from but it rolls over my tongue when I say, "I love you too." I guess the dick and the wine was feeling real good to me.

"I'm glad you feel that way," he says while he was still inside of me. "Because, I want to ask you to be my wife."

I look into his eyes. He's serious.

"Yvette, will you be my wife?"

I think about my miserable life for a moment. I'm lonely, and this fine ass man who can have any bitch he desires wants me instead.

So I exhale, look into his eyes and say, "Yes, Judah. Yes I will marry you. Yes I will be your wife."

CHAPTER 3

MERCEDES

Derrick is in the bedroom sleep, and once again I'm running around with my head chopped off to make things nice for him at home. I know he fucked Bucky, which resulted in me and my friends having to go to court next month, but we're married, and I want to make things work. Not to mention that outside of Yvette, Derrick is the only one who has a tap into Lil C.

When dinner is prepared I call out into our condo. He yawns and walks out. I sit across from him at our dining room table. He's reading one of them mind-power books he loves called, *'The Art Of War'*.

As mad as I get with him, I can never understand why he has to be so sexy? Like even now, he's wearing a white t-shirt, but I can still see the muscles on his chest and arms. Still, we don't fuck on a regular basis. I can't even remember the last time I gave him some pussy. I guess I'm not in the mood these days.

"Derrick, can you sit the book down," I ask. "I want to talk to you. Like a married couple is supposed to."

He sits the book on the table and looks over at me. "What's on your mind, beautiful?"

I love when he calls me that. I can feel my light skin blushing. "Have you talked to Lil C lately?"

He sighs, leans back in the chair and looks at the ceiling. "Mercedes, how come every time we talk, you want the conversation to be about C?"

"Because, he isn't talking to me that's why. But he does talk to you. And Chante misses her brother. I want my family to get back together."

"Mercedes, who are you trying to fool?" Derrick laughs. "Because you and me both know the last thing on Chante's mind these days is Lil C. She's in private school during the week, and when she comes home on the weekends, she's ripping and running the streets with your mother."

He's right, and sometimes I feel bad for the relationship I don't have with my daughter. When Chante was eight years old she was having problems in school. I didn't know what to do with her, and Cameron wasn't helping me, so I put her in a full-time facility for problem children in Virginia. After a year she was doing better, but instead of bringing her home while I was in the middle of the Dreyfus beef, she wanted to stay in the program. I go see her every week, but each time it feels like I don't know her anymore. I guess now that she's thirteen, it's like she wants to do her own thing, and I allow her too.

She has new friends, and I feel like it's no place for me in her life.

Lil C is different. He understands what the drug lifestyle means, and I can relate to him more. But since he found out from Persia that I killed his father, he wants nothing else to do with me.

"Chante does want to spend time with Lil C, and of course I do too," I admit.

"Come over here," He says to me.

I wipe my mouth on the napkin, throw it on the table and walk toward him. I see the way he eyes the blue jeans I'm wearing that hugs my curves. He positions his legs away from the table, grabs my hand and pulls me onto his lap.

"Mercedes, you gotta let C come to you when he's ready. Trust me, C will be there when you need him the most. I know that for a fact. He won't let you down. He loves you too much for that."

This nigga is not saying shit I wanna to hear. Fuck the future. I'm talking about now. "Well what about me? And what I need right now? Don't that count for nothing?"

"You know that it does," he replies. "But he ain't no kid no more, Mercedes. You and Cameron forced him to grow up fast, and that's exactly what he's done. So he can't be controlled anymore. But, you not gonna tell me that he doesn't love you. Just give him the time. There isn't a person on the face of the earth, with a heart anyway, that can deny his own mother forever. He'll come around."

"But I want to hear him say he loves me now," I reply.

"You see what I'm saying?" he asks. "Everything with you is, *I, I, I.*" he stabs me into the softness of my breast with his index finger. "You don't know nothing else. I know what *you* want, but C was close to his father, and he ain't here no more. The boy's hurt that's all."

"Derrick, don't fake like you don't know the nigga wanted me dead."

"If anybody remembers the old times, its me. But that was then and this is now. He feels like you took the one person from him that truly understood him. Let him have a moment to grieve."

"Did he tell you that?"

"Yes," he replies.

"When?"

"Yesterday when we went to the gym."

"You didn't tell me you were seeing C yesterday."

"You didn't ask."

I stand up and walk back toward my seat. Why does everybody but me get to have a relationship with him? I'm the one who pushed him out of my pussy! Not Derrick, and definitely not Yvette. Why am I forced to hear about how he's doing through somebody else? I would even take a business relationship with him if it was possible, and be the one who drops his package, but C refuses to see my face. A face that could look upon him with nothing but love.

"I will do whatever I have to, to have a relationship with my son again," I say honestly. "I don't care what it is."

"Then start by letting him go," he responds.

"I can't."

"Well you will lose him."

"It's not that I don't want to, I don't know how," I reply under my breath. "I don't know how to let my son go. I feel like he still needs me."

"Well that may be the reason you lose him for good," he says picking up his book again.

For some reason, at this moment, I hate Derrick's guts. I know he doesn't want to talk about Lil C anymore, but he's on my mind, and I need some relief. I feel like I don't have Derrick's support. He could bring us together if he really wanted too. I know he could.

Instead of pushing the issue, I think of something else to discuss. "How do you feel about Yvette marrying Judah? She doesn't even know him."

"I don't feel nothing about it," he says turning the page.

I frown. "Can you put the book down please?"

He places the book down, but it's with a slight attitude this time. "I'm trying to talk to you."

"So how about you talk to me about something that has to do with you," he yells.

"I am."

"Damn, Mercedes, lately all anything has been about is Lil C, Yvette, Carissa and Persia. I'm not one of your little girlfriends; I'm your fucking husband. Instead of treating me like one of them bitches, how 'bout you help me a little on this marriage tip. I'm working on it by myself in case you didn't know."

"What is that supposed to mean?"

"When was the last time we fucked?"

My face warms up. "I can't remember."

"Well I do. It's been well over three months since I felt inside of your pussy walls," he responds folding his arms over his chest. "I can't touch my own wife. It's killing me inside."

"Derrick, it ain't like you didn't fuck around on me—,"

"Yes, I fucked that bitch," he yells louder. "And, I know it was wrong for stepping out on our marriage. But don't forget the reason she was able to infiltrate in the first place. You dropped the ball with me. You weren't taking care of me, and playing your position as my wife."

"Yeah, yeah, yeah," I tease. "It was because you hated that the niggas in Emerald City referred to you as Mr. Mercedes. News flash, Derrick. That shit wasn't my fault. You should've stood tall, because at the end of the day, I am your boss, and I come home to you every night."

"It wasn't just about that. It was about you not treating me like a man. I'm starting to tire of this distance shit, Mercedes. But you gonna either have to forgive me or let me go."

My jaw tightens. "Why is this changing over on me all of a sudden? I'm not the one who has stepped outside of the marriage. You are."

"Mercedes, did you take me back just so she couldn't have me? Just so you could torture me?"

I look down. I have never been asked that question before and 'yes' feels like it would be closer to the truth. Instead I say, "No. I'm not even thinking about Bucky anymore."

"Then let's work on us for real," he continues. "Let's spend some quality time together. Let's make love. Let's talk about us having children together. I want a family of my own."

"I don't want no more kids, Derrick," I respond quickly. "You know that."

"You know what, I'm sick of this bullshit," he says standing up.

"Where are you going?"

"To the bathroom," he picks up his book. "Don't worry, if you want to gossip about them bitches you roll with, I can still hear you from in here."

"Fuck you," I yell as he walks away.

"Give me a time and I might show up," he responds before disappearing.

I place my hands over my face and breathe into them. My warm breath moistens my palms and relaxes me. I know he's right about me not doing him right in this marriage, but I hate him. I hate that he stepped out on me with a bitch that banks at the liquor store. I hate that he was going to leave me for her. I hate that had I not caught him, they would've still been together, behind my back. And I hate that my friends know.

He embarrassed me in my own city. It would be different if he was dealing with a boss bitch. Somebody who was contributing to the relationship financially *and* sexually like I do. But he didn't. He chose down and for that I wanted him to pay. Maybe it's time for me to give him a break though. He seems like he's at his limit.

I clean the table off, put the dishes in the dishwasher and walk to the bathroom. Derrick is still inside. I decide to apologize and get serious about my marriage. Maybe if things worked out with us, Lil C would come back so the three of us could be a family. It's obvious he respects Derrick.

I'm about to knock on the door when I hear Derrick talking softly inside. I can't make out what he's saying, so I rush to my bedroom, and walk to my closet. I pull out a half empty shoebox under a stack of filled shoeboxes. Inside is an intercom speaker. Derrick didn't know it, but every room in this house was wired with audio and video equipment, for my viewing and listening pleasure.

I knew what Derrick was doing, and when he was doing it at all times. But after eavesdropping for months, with no new information, I put the speaker up in this box. Now I may be on to something.

I close my closet door and turn the speaker on.

"Nakato, please don't have that nigga's kid," Derrick says. "Don't break my heart with that shit. I think I made a mistake by coming back here. I want to come home to you. I don't even care anymore."

I drop the speaker. I'm devastated. Why does he have to break my heart? I know the name Nakato because it's written on all my paperwork from court. Nakato 'Bucky' Uba is her full name. And, she single handedly ruined my marriage. I can't kill her yet, because the police will know. I'll get at her later though. That I promise.

But I'm done with Derrick. I can't take no more of his lies, of the pain and deceit. He's out of my life for good.

I stand up, grab my purse, and pull out my 9 mili with the silencer attached. I tiptoe toward the closed bathroom door, and fire in the direction I know he's in on the toilet. I hear him gasp for air, but I don't stop shooting. I fire three more times until I hear a thump. Then I rush into the bathroom, and look down at his bloodied body.

I grab the bloody cell phone out of his hands and place it to my ear. "Say something about this shit, Bucky, and you'll find out who I really am, and what kind of person I could really be. I'll see you in court next month," I throw the phone on his bloodied face.

Like I said, I was done with Derrick, but I wasn't about to let her have him either. So he had to go.

CHAPTER 4
LIL C

Lil C was laying flat on his back while Monie rode his dick from the top. They were in the apartment they shared in Tyland Towers. Lil C learned a long time ago from his mother and father that you could manage your kingdom better when you lived in your city, amongst your own people and product. So he ruled it closely and with an iron fist.

C was wearing nothing but the Camelot chain on his neck. And he was in awe at how round Monie's titties were, and how solid her thighs were. Although Monie was thicker than most girls he fucked in the past, there wasn't a one of them who could stand next to Monie's fuck game in the bedroom.

C gripped her plump breasts and fucked her harder. "Damn, Monie," he said biting his bottom lip. "This pussy be right all the time."

"And so do this dick, C," she responded. "I fucking love you so much."

"I know, mami," he replied.

His dick continued to slam into her like fist bumps. He was handling her soggy wetness like a pro. C already stopped himself from cumming twice, because he wanted the feeling to last. Their friendship made the sex even better, to hear him tell it. What better scenario in the world but to fuck your best friend, someone who you could have fun with, and who knew your secrets?

Almost a year ago, Monie had been only a comrade. She rode with him when shit got thick in his pursuit to take over Tyland Towers, now called Camelot. And, she proved that although she was a big girl, she could give him everything them other girls couldn't. That included cooking breakfast, lunch and dinner for him, and fucking him around the clock. C's wish was her command.

C was about to splash his cum into her body until she got up, turned around and rode his dick with her back in his direction. Her phat ass spilled over his thighs like soft pillows. Monie didn't have a cellulite spot on her body. She was all muscular shiny ass, and he could no longer last.

"Fuck," he called out into their home.

"Keep it stiff for one more second," Monie begged as she focused her attentions on getting her nut off. Since C had gotten his, she knew she needed to hurry or she would be short, and left playing with her vibrator. With a few more waist tilts, and three more plops onto his dick, she spilled her milk all over him.

"Damn, Monie," C said pulling out of her. "Your pussy shouldn't be that good all the time."

Monie lifted off of him and lie next to him in their bed. "I'm glad you liked it. It was good for me too." Her mood was cold and short.

"Well why you don't seem like it was good? You sound dry. Like I just beat you in Spades and shit."

"No reason," she sighed.

There was something sad aback her eyes. C wanted her to be happy, truly he did, so he pulled himself together and decided to investigate the reason for her dismay.

"What's on your mind, Monie? Come out with it." He wiped his dick with the white towel on the nightstand, and threw it on the floor. When he accidently looked at her plump breasts he was hardening up again. He could fuck some more if she was willing. But, now was not the time. So he thought about his comrades and got soft again. He wanted to give her his undivided attention, and he knew she would get mad if he went in for some more of that crucial.

"It ain't nothing, C" she lied pulling the sheets over her naked body. The curved brown sheets outlined her nipples, and the roundness of her sexy body. "I'm good."

"We been friends too long for you to lie to me," he admitted. "Now stop fucking around. What's on your mind?"

"That's just it, C," she said softly. "I don't want to be your friend anymore. I love you too much for that shit. I mean, you got me in your apartment, you sleep with me every night, and yet you still see other bitches on the side. I want an official position."

"But I've never disrespected you have I?" C questioned. "I've never brought one of my females here, and you the only one I fuck raw. You set up like a queen, Monie, accept you're the closest thing to me, we better than the dumb shit. Lets not mince words by adding name tags."

Monie sighed. "C, I don't know how much longer I can be with you like this," she said. "You asked for my body, but you stole my heart instead. If you want a roommate than I'm cool with that, but I don't want to sleep in your bed anymore without knowing you're mine."

C frowned. "So I guess you gonna pay rent then too? I got an extra bedroom."

"C, I'm serious."

He jumped up. "Fuck," he yelled throwing his arms up in the air. "What do you want from me? I mean, you're the first bitch I—,"

"I'm not a bitch, C," Monie said sitting up in the bed. "I'm the one who loves you more than you can love yourself. All I'm asking is that you love me back."

"And I do," he said. "Just not in the way you want me too."

"You're spoiled, C. You use to having everything you want. All your life doors have been kicked down for you, but what you gotta hurt me in the process."

"You're right, I am spoiled. And that's not gonna change just cause you asking it too."

When the phone rings Monie reached over on the nightstand and answered it. "Hello."

Silence.

"Who is this?" Monie said. When no one responded she hung up. "You know that was the bitch Persia again. I don't know why you won't just let me beat that baby out of her, and be done with it. You know Monie official with the hands." She laughed at herself. "Plus if you ask me, the baby probably ain't even yours."

Monie eased out of the bed and when she did, C was in her face. "I had one of the best fathers in the world, before my mother took him away from me. He was honorable and he always did the right thing by me and my sister."

"What you saying?" Monie asked.

"I'm saying if she's carrying my seed, I'm gonna do right by her and the baby," he said. "And that means I'm not gonna allow anybody to hurt one of my kid's parents, the way my mother did me. In order for a kid to be full he needs both parents in his life, Monie. So, if she is carrying my kid she will always be okay. You understand what I'm saying? She's off limits, and I won't let you hurt her."

"You might be doing the right thing," Monie said. "But you need to put Persia on to what's going on up in here too. Because, the bitch thinks she can still be with you, C. And it's only a matter of time before she starts with her old games again. She's dangerous. Mark my words."

"Let me handle Persia," he walked away from her. "I just want you to know that if you gonna be in

my life, you gonna have to put your feelings about that matter to the side."

Monie slumped on the bed in defeat. "Speaking of parents, how come you haven't spoken to your mother yet? You hold a grudge longer than me."

"I'm gonna tell you like I told everybody else, let me handle my business when it comes to them peoples."

"Them peoples is your mother, your flesh and blood. You rapping about needing both parents yet you acting like you ain't got one still alive."

"It's my business, Monie. Not yours. If I want your opinion I'll tell you."

Monie threw her hands up in the air and leaned back on the bed. When the phone rang again she reluctantly answered.

"Hello."

"Monie, I need you to tell C to come to my house right away," Mercedes yelled. "It's urgent."

CHAPTER 5
CARISSA

The smell of the wooden cherry dining room table, in one of the apartments within the Black Water Klan's headquarters, I was sitting at, made my stomach churn. I'm supposed to be eating the steak, white rice and eggs that they made me for dinner, but I don't trust anyone here. Why would I? At one point in history they tried to kill us, and they succeeded at killing one of my best friends...Kenyetta. She was also the only person on the face of the earth who I could truly relate too. She knew my secrets, we snorted coke together, and we partied hard. I miss her so much.

And now here I am, begging for mercy from someone I don't know, so that I can maintain a relationship with a daughter who hates me. I feel like a traitor.

Persia is on the other side of the table, sitting next to Karen. She's wearing a red t-shirt with a large white teddy bear on the front. They must be buying her clothes, because she would've never purchased something that makes her look so young, and ridiculous. Why does this have to be the only way I see my daughter? I know me and Persia have had our problems in the past, but we still family. Why does she hate me so?

"Your sister misses you," I say to Persia. I fork through my rice, as opposed to eating it. "All she talks about everyday is Persia this, and Persia that."

Persia rolls her eyes at me. "Cut the shit, ma. You and me both know that Treasure can't stand me, and I can't stand her," she opens a jar of jalapenos and pours them onto her steak. That can't be good for the baby.

"She does miss you."

"Whatever, about this time she should be experimenting with sex by licking her friend Bria's pussy. She's eleven years old now anyway. At least that's what me and my homie did when we played alone."

"Persia," I scream at her. "Why would you say something so vile about your sister?"

Persia laughs at me. "Why you mad? Aunt Yvette a dyke! A little pussy licking never hurt nobody, you should try it."

I move toward her but Karen stands up and yells, "Oscar, come here." She's holding the red bible looking thing in her hand, and I wonder what's in its pages.

I stay where I am. They took my gun so I'm not strapped. I don't feel safe here.

Oscar, who I saw the first day I met Karen, comes running into the room. "What's wrong, ma?" he pushes his glasses to his face. "Are you okay?"

"Yes. Take Persia out of here." Karen looks at me. "I need to talk to her mother alone."

Oscar looks at me once more, before he leaves the room with my daughter. When they are gone Karen and I are standing alone in front of one another.

"He's going to take her as his wife," Karen says to me sitting back in her chair. "He'll do right by her too. Trust me, me and Black Water raised him right. The kind of man he is they don't make no more."

I lean in. "What do you mean take her as his wife?"

"She's still young," Karen says plainly. "And although she's been spoiled once with that baby, she can have more. *Many more*. We just have to indoctrinate her into our ways and customs, and work on her selfish spirit. I have my hands full no doubt, but I'm sure it will be worth it."

My heart rate increases. I don't want my daughter here. I don't want her to be indoctrinated and I definitely don't want her to be promised to some crazed teenager as his wife. I want her home. I want to comb her hair, and pretend to get irritated with her when she steals my clothes. I want to walk down the street with her, arm and arm, as fresh little boys flirt and look her way. I want to tell her about life, and make-believe that I'm smart enough to know what to do when times get rough. I want to love her, and most of all I want to protect her.

But I can't do that now. I have to pretend to not see what's going on. I have to pretend that I don't know that if things keep going the way that they are,

I will never see my daughter outside of these walls again. And, she'll most likely be brainwashed like all of these people.

"Karen, I don't know what Persia has told you, but she is not ready to marry anybody. She's very immature. I mean did you see her just now? Did you hear what she just said?"

"Carissa, take a seat."

I don't.

"Please sit."

I sit down, and she does too.

"Please don't worry about Persia," she crosses her legs. "We won't legally marry her off until she's eighteen." She grips that red book she always carries. What's in that thing anyway?

"*Legally*?"

"Yes, although our young girls can't marry until eighteen, they take husbands before that time." Karen folds her hands on the table, over the red book. "Persia, has expressed to us an interest to be a part of who we are, and welcome our traditions."

"And what exactly are your traditions?"

"We stand by each other, and we live by our word."

"Is your word Christian? Or Catholic?" I ask. I'm trying to hide my irritation but I know I'm doing a poor job.

She laughs. "Our tradition is steep within *our* word." She rubs the book. "And unless you are a part of who we are, I'm not at liberty to discuss what we believe with you."

"Karen, please listen to me, you have to forgive me for not being totally comfortable with this situation. I want to come at you from one mother to another. Can I?"

"Proceed."

"Your son and the other people here may have been raised in your beliefs, and I won't try to come in the way of that. But, as you can see Persia is angry, and very immature. She wouldn't know the first thing about what to do with a husband, let a lone a man or awkward traditions. If you keep her here she will shake up your foundation, I swear before God."

"Why do you say that?"

"Did you see the way she just behaved?"

"Yes I did, Carissa," she says. "But she has every right to be angry. I've spent quite a bit of time talking to her about her family life."

I lean back in my seat and frown at her. "And just what do you think that you know about me and my life?"

"For starters I am aware that you and your friends have operated a drug business in Emerald City all of her life. Since she's been in your care she's seen cocaine, weed and what she described as yellow gold on a consistent basis. She has also expressed to me that she's aware of key people who were murdered in her family, including but not limited to, her uncle Cameron who was Mercedes' fiancé. So believe me when I say I know a lot about you and your family's lifestyle."

"So ya'll don't deal in coke? Or heroin? Don't fake, Karen."

"That's not what I'm saying."

I am so angry with Persia right now I could kill her. That's how I know she's not ready for this life. Why would she tell somebody about what we do behind Emerald City's walls? Her disloyalty is paramount and makes me shiver. I raised that girl. She came from my body. So why is she not built like I am?

"You're right, she's seen a lot, a whole lot," a tear falls down my face and I swipe it off. "But she grew up on my bullshit." I look around the dining room that we're sitting in. There's a picture of Black Water on the wall. He's posing like Jesus, except he has a gold chain hanging around his neck. "But this is all new bullshit that my daughter is not accustomed to."

"And yet here we are," Karen replies. "Carissa, I have no doubt that you and Yvette are probably use to running things in Emerald City, but around here I am boss. I am Lord." Her eyes seem to twinkle when she makes that statement. She loves the power like Yvette. I'm sure of it.

"You can't have my daughter," I say flat out. "I won't let you have her. I have lost everything recently. The love of my life, my best friend and my sanity. I don't know who I will be if I lose one of my kids too."

"You've already lost your daughter," Karen smirks. "Can't you see that yet?"

"It's not my fault that you and Yvette don't have a relationship."

She frowns. "What do you think you know about me and Yvette?"

"I know that your eyes lit up when you first saw her face. And I know that your heart seemed broken when you thought she had a relationship with your mother and you didn't. I get all of that, but you can't blame me for that situation. It isn't my fault. So please don't try to make me pay for it, by stealing my first born."

Karen stands up and walks toward the door. "Be careful, Carissa. I'm the only person standing between the relationship you want with your oldest daughter, and the relationship you don't have. Now either we can get along, and be the best of friends, or I can make things difficult for you."

"How much do you want?"

She grins. "A lot. When you murdered Tamir, we lost a load of money in the process. And although we own two of our buildings, the taxes are steep. So, you take care of us financially, and I'll keep the peace between you and your child."

"How much?" I repeat.

"Three hundred thousand dollars."

"That's a lot of money."

"Is Persia worth it? Only you can answer that."

I hate this bitch so much. "How do I know you won't stab me in the back? If I pay you?"

"Because I'm tired of fighting, Carissa. Since Black Water has led the war against Emerald City, a lot of good people have been killed. I just want to keep my family together and live by his will." She looks at Black Water's picture.

"You haven't answered my question, how do I know I can trust you?"

"Because you don't have a choice. I'm holding the cards, not you." Karen walks toward the door, with the red book. "You can let yourself out." When she opens the door an armed guard is on the other side. "And when you finish your meal, he'll escort you to make sure you get out of the building safe. No offense, but you're not very popular around here. Somebody might kill you to score points with the Klan." She closes the door and leaves me alone.

I bawl into tears and my stomach aches. All I want to do is the line of coke I have stuffed in my bag. I'm about to do it on the cherry table, when my cell phone rings. It's Yvette's number.

"Carissa, you have to meet us at Mercedes' house. Something fucked up has happened."

"I'm on my way."

CHAPTER 6
YVETTE

I make it to Mercedes' door and remove the key from my pocket to let myself inside. Once I'm in I see Carissa, Mercedes and Toi in the living room. Don't get me wrong. I fuck with Toi. *Hard*. She's a cool girl. But, this is personal business.

When we needed help to lure Cameron to be killed, Toi, who was his girlfriend at the time, helped us murder him. When we beat Bucky's ass in the Laundromat, Toi got some licks in too. Toi was also the person to show us the video that was being shown around DC of Carissa fucking some dude, because of her love for porn she found it. So I like her, it's just that I don't know if I like her enough to have her in on *every* illegal thing we do. But Mercedes feels otherwise. She trusts her too much.

"Thank god you're here," Mercedes says hugging me. "I'm so sorry about this shit, girl. I snapped and one thing led to another. This nigga was foul though, Yvette. He had to go. I'm not letting another nigga do me wrong. I just can't."

She releases me and I lock the door. I look at the middle of the living room floor, and see Derrick's corpse lying on a red and gold Gucci shower curtain. He's wearing bullet holes to the chest, and his face is frozen in a horror position. It's like he saw a ghost before he died. Maybe he did. Six hacksaws are lying around his body and I know what they are for. Chop work.

I look at Toi and say, "What are you doing here?"

Toi looks behind herself, and then back at me. "You talking to me?" She points to herself.

"What you think?"

"What do you mean what I'm doing here? Mercedes called, and I came."

"Do you really think you can handle this type of lifestyle?" I question. "I hear you still work at the Social Security Administration in Baltimore city. Clocking in at nine and out at five."

"So."

"So we ain't them type bitches. We gangsters. And, I got a feeling you outside of your league."

"Yvette, what are you doing?" Mercedes interrupts. "Why you coming at Toi like that, considering everything she has done for us? You act like she hasn't proven to be true blue already."

"Scoot back some, Mercedes. Toi a big girl," I remind her. "She can answer the question for herself."

"You don't know shit about me, home girl," Toi says.

"Fuck that supposed to mean?"

"I might not wear my stripes on my sleeve, but it don't make me a square. Sometimes it's not about showcasing the things that you've done, but keeping the secrets of the things you got away with."

"Still not sure this lifestyle is for you," I say.

"Yvette, I don't know what lifestyle you're referring to, but I don't play when it comes to my friends. Mercedes called me frantic when I was at the movies with my boyfriend, so I dropped everything and came here. I mean what you trying to get at? That I'm a snitch?"

I face Mercedes. "You can't replace Kenyetta, Mercedes. I don't care how many fly bitches you roll with, not one of them will be able to stand next to Kenyetta." I focus back on Toi. "Not even you."

Toi places her hands on her hips and smirks. "I don't know what your mind is over there creating, but I gotta agree with you on one thing. I could never replace Kenyetta, because I don't want too. I'm in my own lane and on my own highway. It's funny to me that this is coming up all of a sudden though. You act like I've never put in work with ya'll before."

"You're right about that, you could never replace my best friend. She was a ride or die bitch who stood strong until the day she died. And, it's important that you know that."

"Mercedes, maybe I should go," Toi says grabbing her black MCM purse.

"Please don't leave, Toi," Mercedes responds wiping the tears away that stream down her face.

"I have to," Toi replies. "Shit is getting thick in here, and you need to be in the right state of mind for whatever you're about to do with this nigga's body."

"Yvette, this shit is dumb," Mercedes says to me. "I need all of my friends by my side right now."

"And you'll have them once she leaves," I look at Toi.

Toi moves toward the door with an attitude.

Before she disappears I say, "I trust you won't say anything about what you've seen here tonight." I look at Derrick's corpse. "I don't know if Mercedes ever mentioned it to you before, but I can be evil if me or mines is fucked with."

I don't know how she did it but in a second flat she was up in my face. "Don't threaten me, Yvette. I don't like threats."

"Toi, maybe you should go," Mercedes says to her with her gun aimed at the back of Toi's head. "And do it quick."

Toi turns around and looks at Mercedes. "So you pull your weapon out on me, when you called me here for help?"

"Call it a reflex," Mercedes says. "Now bounce. I'll get up with you later."

Toi eventually leaves the apartment, and the three of us are alone. It's not like I need any confirmation about Mercedes' loyalty, but that move proved to me even more where Mercedes' heart lies. I know how she feels about Toi.

"I hate you for that shit, Yvette," Mercedes says tossing her gun on the couch. "Toi is real people, and you may have fucked that up for me. Some people can't meet one real person in a lifetime, and I was blessed to meet four."

"If she is as real as you say she is, she'll be able to get past that shit. She'll understand business is business, and everybody got a place." I walk up to Derrick's corpse. "Now what happened? Why this nigga dead?"

Mercedes sighs. "It's a long story," she looks down at him. "But, I need to wait for C before I explain everything."

"C ain't coming, Mercedes. He called me, and when I told him that we were on our way too, he decided not to show up. He knows we can handle the situation, so ain't no need in him getting involved. We deal with this type shit all of the time."

Her eyes widen. "What…why?"

"Because he doesn't want a relationship with you," I yell. "You know that already. Don't you?" Suddenly something dawns on me. I walk closer to Mercedes. "Wait a minute, did you kill Derrick thinking that Lil C would be there for you, and your relationship would be repaired?"

Sorrow washes from her face. She's angry now. "What the fuck are you talking about, Yvette?" She walks away from me and sits on the sofa. "You talking dumb now. I killed this mothafucka because he had it coming. Living in my house. Sleeping in my bed. Eating my food. Playing in my pussy. And, still fucking with that bitch? This how he do me? Fuck that shit, not on my watch."

I walk closer to her and stare down at her head. "Mercedes, did you kill him trying to make Lil C feel sorry for you?"

"Yvette, I called Lil C out of reflex. And because he's my son. Nothing more, nothing less."

"C loved Derrick, and you called him without even considering what this would mean to see him like this. That's selfish on fifty levels, 'Cedes. You acting like a child now. C is not Cameron he is your boy-child-man."

"You didn't think about what it would mean to me either," Carissa says with an attitude. "I was meeting with Persia before you called. You know this bitch Karen is milking us for our money. The least you could do is allow me the time I need to spend with her."

"Carissa, ain't nobody thinking about Persia's stink-box ass."

"Bitch, that's my daughter you talking about," Carissa yells.

"Exactly, but this situation right here ain't about you, or her," Mercedes replies. "You turned it into that. Now you can leave if you want too. It ain't like you been here for me when I needed you anyway. The only thing on your mind these days is Persia. You barely help us around Emerald anymore. But when it comes time for the split on the cash, you be on that like flies on shit. Talking 'bout where my fifty, where my fifty."

"And the only thing on your mind not your son?" Carissa asks her. "You act like Chante ain't even in the building anymore. You threw her in private school and pretty much washed your hands of her when Cameron died. I bet you that nigga rolling over in his grave right now for the way you treating his daughter. One day Chante gonna come at you hard too. Get ready."

Mercedes jumped up and accidently stepped on Derrick's stiff hand. "Bitch, don't tell me shit about my daughter. If anything you the one who has abandoned Treasure. Far as I can see you don't get the mother of the year award neither, so sit your flat ass down somewhere."

I can't believe it. Although I should I can't believe that these two are still fighting each other. After everything we've been through, you'd think they'd understand that in this world, all we got is each other.

They're yelling at the top of their lungs, so I pull my gun out, and fire another bullet into Derrick's corpse. They're quiet now.

"Listen, if you ask me both of you bitches are tripping," I say to them. "You're letting your kids control everything you do, and they don't give a fuck about how either of you feel about it neither. Now I need you to pull yourselves together, and lets chop down this body. Because I don't know if ya'll remember or not, but the Vanishers have been missing in action for a minute, and dumping this body is our priority alone."

They stop arguing and we all stand in the middle of the floor, observing Derrick's body. Damn, Derrick. He was the last nigga of the original Emerald City squad, and now he's gone.

"Mercedes, I don't know why you did this shit," I say to her. "To be honest, I don't even care. You could walk up to a catholic priest, and shoot him in the head, and I'll still have your back. Because I love you, and you're my friend. But if you killed this nigga to get at C, this gonna come back on you again. This some bad karma type shit. This nigga was loved. Be prepared for that."

"I'm so confused right now," Mercedes says to herself.

"I hate you lately, Mercedes," Carissa says, "but I feel the same way Yvette does. No matter what you do, I'll have your back. Always. Just don't make no moves like this again without putting us on. Killing should be our last priority, not the first."

Mercedes' eyes widen. "Damn, bitch," she says looking at Carissa. "I didn't think you had any love for me left in your heart."

"Then I guess you don't know me no more. Maybe that's my fault. Maybe it's both of our faults. I guess its true what they say, you can't pick your family members. We stuck together for life." Carissa grabs a hacksaw, drops to her knees and begins sawing off Derrick's arm. "But I do have a question for you, did you really do this thinking C would come back into your life?"

Mercedes grabs another hacksaw and says, "You would've done the same thing. Wouldn't you?"

CHAPTER 7
MERCEDES

Derrick had to die. I know it's messed up the way I did it, but I had my reasons. The fucked up part was that I didn't get what I wanted, a relationship with my son. So now I'm at his condominium at Tyland Towers, planning to make him speak to me.

Before knocking on his door, I take two deep breaths. When I'm strong enough, I knock firmly.

"Just a minute," someone says inside.

When the door opens I see Monie. She's way chunkier than the girls I've seen C with, so I wonder how she roped him. What makes her so special?

She's wearing grey sweatpants, and a plain white t-shirt. I don't know how to take this girl now that she and C are together. When she use to come over my house with C, I thought she was loud-mouthed and rude. I wonder what happened to bring them together.

A smile spreads across her face as she looks at me. "Oh my, god," she says smoothing her ponytail backwards. "Had I known you were coming I would've freshened up. I'm so sorry."

She's pretty. I never noticed it before but she's an attractive girl and there is something genuine about her. I like her already, although I want to know a little more about her, especially if she's with my son.

"Don't worry about freshening up, unless you don't intend on letting me in," I tell her.

She laughs heavily, opens the door wider and backs up. "I'm tripping now, Ms. Mercedes. Please forgive me. Come inside. C isn't home though."

I'm disappointed at his absence.

When I walk into their apartment I'm impressed. The living room is very spacious and the furnishings are bright and welcoming. The kitchen cabinets and counters are white lacquer and shine brightly. I smell Pine-sol. Looks like the young girl knows how to keep house, another check in her direction. If she keeps this up I might be Team Monie.

"Can I get you something to drink?" she asks me.

I sit on the sofa. "What do you have?"

"Wine…beer…liquor," she says.

"Bring me a little of all three."

She smiles. "It's been one of those days huh?"

"No doubt."

She goes to fulfill my order and brings back my drinks. I notice a box of Argo Starch on the able with a spoon inside. She must be eating that shit. She sits them on the glass table, and I start with the red wine. "You're too fat," I say to her sipping my drink. "And if you want to keep C, you'll have to lose a lot of weight. Now you might not be willing to do that, and that's okay if you're comfortable with your size. But, I know C, and he's vain. He'll never put you on his arm in public, unless you change."

Her shoulders slump forward, and she plops down next to me on the couch. "I know." She sighs. "I don't want to be like this. And if I thought it would keep him, I wouldn't eat another thing in my life just to lose the weight."

"See that's where you fuck up," I say finishing my wine, and sitting the glass on the table. "You need to lose weight to get what you want, not to get C. I raised him and I know what he desires. He likes a woman with confidence. You gotta act like you want to change, to better yourself, not to rope him. And stop eating that shit, it fattens you up quicker than a ton of ice cream."

"It's done. But what I do want is C," she says. "He ain't trying to hear it though. He thinks just because he moved me in, and I get to answer his phone, that that's enough to appease me. But I want more, Ms. Mercedes. I want a relationship. Am I wrong for wanting him in my life?"

"C is a wonderful young man," I say. "I have loved him all of his life too. So much so, that I fear I might have neglected my daughter in the process. I gotta work on that. But it's like without C in my life, I feel like I'm not complete. He reminds me of his father so much. So to answer your question….no. No you aren't crazy for wanting him in your life.

But how far are you willing to go to get him is the question."

I think about how I killed Derrick to win his love back, and sigh.

Monie looks me in my eyes and says, "For C's love, I'll go as far as I need too."

"Then I'll help you out," I say. "But you gotta help me too."

"Anything."

"I need you to help me repair the relationship with C on your end. You're here with him everyday. You're around him all of the time. Whenever you can, plant a seed in my name. I need your help because nothing I do on the outside works."

"Can we keep things real with each other?"

"Of course, Monie," I respond. "I wouldn't come at you like this if I wasn't going to keep it real."

"It's like this, C resents you for killing his father. If you come at him the right way, and tell him that you really are sorry for what you did, I think he'll welcome the relationship over time. He misses you, I know he does. The other day when I was making him pancakes, I walked into the room to tell him they were almost done. I saw him looking at your picture. And another time I overheard him telling somebody in Emerald City to always watch your back, because he was concerned about the Black Water people. He loves you, he just ain't ready to show it right now that's all."

I feel like I want to cry, but I won't. It feels so good to know that he loves me, even if it's from a far.

"I took the blame for his father's death already," I admit. "But it's like he not listening to me. He doesn't care that I'm sorry for what I did. All he wants me to do is disappear, and to never reach out again."

"I talk to C about you all of the time, Ms. Mercedes. But, he real proud about his father, and if I'm being honest, he's messed up about Derrick too. He was fucked up when he found out he was killed. Even if I could get through to him right now, the Derrick thing sent him further over the edge. I think he needs a little more time."

"Well if he would've came to my house he would've found out why I had to kill him."

"The way he was acting I don't know if any reason would've worked for him," Monie says.

"That nigga raped me," I lie. "You telling me that don't count for nothing? I had to kill him."

The moment I let such a heinous lie fly out of my mouth, I want to suck it back. But how could I? I said it already. I would've never thrown a rape on Derrick's name if he was a real nigga, but he's dirt to me. And it hurt my feelings that when I needed C the most, he didn't show up. But now I'm not ready to nurture that lie.

"Oh my, god," Monie says covering her mouth. "What…I…mean, are you okay?" She examines me.

I feel ashamed. "I'm fine."

"We gotta tell C."

I want the relationship with my son, but I don't want it like that. "I'll be fine," I tell her. "Don't say nothing to C about this, please. I'm trusting you." I smile and tap her knee. "Right now I want to get you where you need to be so you can get what you want, my son."

"Anyway you could help me would be appreciated, Ms. Mercedes."

"I got you." When the phone rings she frowns. "Ain't you gonna get that?" I ask.

"No, it's probably Persia's bitch ass again." She covers her mouth. "Excuse my language, Ms. Mercedes. It's just that I can't stand that worrisome bitch. She's been torturing me ever since she found out we were living together. Today alone she's called fifty times."

"Well get the phone," I frown. "This your house."

"C told me I couldn't go at her," she glares at the phone. "Said if she pregnant, and that's his baby, I'll have to learn to get along with her. I don't see how that's gonna happen because I'm still feeling some kind of way about what she did to you and C's relationship. She ain't have no business telling him about his father, and how he met his demise. That was family business."

I stand up and walk toward the phone. "You might not be able to say anything to the bitch, but I can." I pick up the handset. "Hello."

"Fuck you, you fat ass bitch. While you over there cooking, C just left from eating my pussy. Think about that."

"Persia, this is Mercedes."

Silence.

I guess she wasn't expecting me to answer.

"What are you doing over there?" Persia says in a low voice. "He don't love you no more. I saw to it when I told him what you did to his father."

Her mouth spills venom, so I'll do the same. "Don't worry about all that, just let me say this, C will never want you. Ever," I say. "You're nothing but a washed up little girl who he told me has a funky box, and an even worst dick sucking game. Now my son is going to marry Monie, and they are going to have a wonderful life."

I hear her suck in air, and I realize I just snatched her heart out with my statement.

"Oh yes, it's true, baby doll. Monie is five minutes from royalty, and there ain't nothing you can do about it. So do yourself a favor, go somewhere and hang yourself. It's over for you around here anyway." I end the call.

"I can't believe you just did that," Monie says to me. "C is going to go off if she tells him."

"It's clear that he doesn't want to have anything else to do with me anyway, Monie. I might as well help you out. Fuck Persia's raunchy ass." I feel like a teenager again, but fuck it.

Monie smiles brightly. "Thank you, Ms. Mercedes. I really appreciate it."

"Don't worry about it. I did a favor for you, and maybe one day you can pay it forward."

CHAPTER 8
PERSIA

"Die, die, die," Persia screamed as she punched herself in the belly with both fists. "I want you to die, baby! Come out of me and die!"

When her stomach aches so much her back hurts, she threw herself on the bed and looked up at the ceiling.

"C, please don't do this to me," Persia cried to herself. "Please don't marry that fat toad. She not as cute as me. She don't love you like me. She never will. Nobody will."

When her cell phone rings and she sees it's her mother, she answered it with an attitude. Normally she ignores the phone, but now she wanted to talk to someone who loved her more than she loved them back.

"Mommy, please help me," Persia performed. "Please, mommy."

"What's wrong, baby?" Carissa yelled in fear. "Are you hurt? Are they fucking with you? I'll kill everybody over that mothafucka. Just say the word and my soldiers are there in a heartbeat."

"No, mommy," she sobbed. "It's Aunt Mercedes. She was mean to me. I was in my room, and she called out of nowhere and said that my baby wasn't C's. But, it is C's baby. I ain't never fucked no boy or sucked no boy's dick before I did C's."

"Persia..."

"I'm sorry, mommy but I'm so mad right now. I hate her. I hate her so much. She the reason C don't want to talk to me. She's ruining me!"

"Stop crying, Persia," Carissa said softly. "I'll handle Mercedes. Nobody is gonna disrespect my daughter, not even her own aunt."

"Do you promise, mommy? Because if you promise I'll try harder to have a better relationship with you. I won't curse at you no more or nothing like that. I just want you to go in on aunt Mercedes first. Please."

"Baby, there is nothing more in the world that I want then to have a better relationship with you."

"Then call her and cuss her out," Persia persisted. "Do it now too."

"Okay, let me go find out what's going on, and I'll call you right back."

"That's good, mommy. I love you."

After she finished with her mother, Persia hung up and lied on her bed. She felt good knowing that Carissa was going to give Mercedes what she deserved. Now she had to call C to give him a piece of her mind.

"What?" Lil C said when he answered his cell phone.

"C, I know you don't love me no more."

"Never loved you."

"Whatever, but you need to know your mother cursed me out and I almost had a miscarriage. They had to take me to the hospital and everything. Your baby almost died in my belly."

"When was this?" he asked plainly.

"Earlier today. I'm just getting home now."

C laughed. "I don't know what went down between you and my moms, but I can promise you that you didn't go to no hospital today."

"What...why you say that?"

"Persia, I had somebody watching that building from the day I found out that you were pregnant with my kid, and living there. I keep a set of eyes on you at all times. So believe me when I say you ain't been to no hospital. You haven't even been out of the building. Now if you lying about that shit, you probably lying about my moms calling you out too. So do me a favor, don't call unless you squeezing out my kid.

"And while I'm at it, stop fucking with Monie too. She's being a real sport by not going off on you. But make no mistake, Monie's a gangster, so I advise you to fall back. I'm out."

When C hung up she threw her phone across the room. She was determined to come up with a plan to have them all dealt with. Whatever she decided, she knew it would have to be final.

CHAPTER 9
KAREN

"Ma, I know you have this situation with Carissa and them under control, but I'm still worried that this may cause us problems in the future. We should not be working with them in any way."

Karen leaned back in her black leather chair and looked at her son. He was standing at the other side of her black lacquer desk. His navy blue eyeglasses rested against his face.

"If you say you realize I have things under control, then why are you worried?"

"The Emerald City crew has been harming this family since thy God Black Water was alive. Now we have one of their members in our home, and I don't think it's okay to allow the Emerald City Squad inside, to roam within our walls. They're angry. And when people are angry, they are dangerous."

"Have you forgotten the reason that Persia is here?" Karen asked him. "You wanted Persia as your wife, when I wanted to kill her when Tamir died and left her here, you begged me not to, saying that we could always use another woman to bare

children. So my son, you need to be thanking me for my hospitality, instead of arguing with me."

"And I do thank you, mother. But I never thought you would allow them into our home. Persia is different; in the end she will be one of us. But Carissa and her people will never be good for us."

"Things are going to be fine, son. We have what they want. The girl." Karen paused. "And let's not forget that making this agreement with the Emerald City squad allows us the money we need to keep things going. Until we can find another hustle."

"But me and the boys are already working on a few things," Oscar said.

"And those things might pay off later, but they aren't doing shit for us now," Karen responded. "We don't have Tamir anymore to supply our needs. We need their money."

"It's still a bad move, ma," Oscar persisted. "Black Water would have never approved of this."

"Do you know where Black Water and Tamir went wrong, son?"

"Blasphemy," Oscar said with an attitude. "Black Water didn't go wrong anywhere and I'm ashamed to hear you say that. If one of the family members heard you speak in such ways, they would have you killed for treason."

"Luckily I'm just talking to my son, someone who can keep my secrets right?" When he doesn't answer she gets louder. "You'll keep my secrets right, son?"

"Yes, ma," he said under his breath.

"Good. Now Black Water was a great leader, and his son Tamir was on his way to being the greatest too. But he messed up when he didn't stand close to the doctrine we live by. We were always taught that when possible, we should keep the peace, and I've done that by this arrangement I have with the Emerald City Squad. As much as I loved Tamir and Black Water, they are both dead. This family is not, and it's my responsibility to protect it."

"Are you soft because you found out about your sister?"

Karen sits up in her chair and stares her son directly into the eyes. She's beyond insulted because he knows first hand the people she has killed. He knows her murderous heart.

"You've known me all of your life, and you can still ask me that question? The only reason you're still standing is because I gave birth to you. But, I'm not sure that I will extend the same graces to you if you disrespect me in that way again."

"I'm just trying to make sense of this," he said. "I didn't mean to disrespect you."

"Well it's too late for that, Oscar. You already have. And let me give you a warning. If you ever come at me like that again I will forget that you are my child. Now leave me alone."

When he left Karen removed a small silver key from the desk. She walked across the room to a large black chest against the wall. She pulled out a large red leather book that resembled a bible. She walked it over to her seat, sat down and placed the book on top of the desk.

Karen flipped open the book and stopped on page five. Inside were the laws and 100 Commandments in Black Water's handwriting. She placed her finger on the first commandment.

She read them out loud.

"Man should put no man before the Klan. Number two, man should do all he can to protect the Klan. Number three, unless otherwise impossible, man should keep the peace if it benefits the Klan. Number four; if the enemy sees peace as a weakness, man should bring down that enemy by extreme force. Number five, man should consider the heart but always be seeking power. Number six, to preserve the Klan, all members must breed."

Having gotten a refresher on what the Klan stood for, she felt right by making a decision to deal with the Pitbulls. Her only wish was that her son would see things the same way as she did.

When she was done wit the doctrine, she picked the book back up, walked it over to the chest and locked it up. When she was done she returned the key, slid out of her office, and closed the door.

Karen was in her head so she didn't see Persia hiding in the shadows of the hallway. Originally Persia was going to cry to Karen, by telling her all of the things that Mercedes said to her over the phone. Now she had a better idea. If Oscar believed that Karen was being soft by not defending Tamir and Black Water's legacies, she decided to play on that newfound information.

But first she wanted to see what was in that book.

CHAPTER 10

YVETTE

I'm sitting on my living room sofa thinking about my life. Carissa's mouth is moving but I don't hear her voice. I got too much shit on my mind, and heart. I think I'm making a mistake by marrying Judah. I don't love him. I barely like him. He seems manufactured, like somebody God gave me just to appease me and answer my prayers.

The saddest part is that I'm holding a secret that I will never tell my friends out loud. I'm still thinking of Thick. I never *fully* got over him I suppose.

When he was alive as mean as he was, he limited the things I had to do. I didn't have to say where I was going to live, he told me. I didn't have to say where I wanted to go to eat, he told me. I didn't have to ponder what to think, he thought for me. Since I killed him I've been sitting around like one of them bobble-head dolls I see in car windows. I'm lost.

"...So if she gonna act like that, Yvette, I'll just put it to her ass. She not gonna keep disrespecting my daughter though. Believe that shit. Mercedes thinks just because she loud she can do what she wants to other people's kids. Fuck that shit, you hear me?"

"Tell her that when she gets here," I say sipping my wine. "I'm sure she'll have a response for you."

When my glass is empty, I stand up. I'm about to open my last bottle of Merlot, in my kitchen. On the way back, I walk past my bedroom door. My dogs are barking wildly in my room, and they sound angry with me. I hate that I have to put them up when company comes over, but everybody's scared of them. I feel like I'm being disloyal, and I hate that feeling of disloyalty.

I'm almost in the kitchen when I hear a car outside. I turn around and walk back to the door. When I push my yellow curtain to the side, I see Mercedes' gold Benz pull up in the front of my house, I'm certain that this evening is not going to end right. I sit my empty glass on the end table by the door, and let her inside.

"Where that bitch at?" Mercedes asks busting into my house.

"Hello, Mercedes," I say. I close the door, and she walks up to Carissa.

"Say that shit you was talking over the phone to my face, Carissa." Mercedes throws her purse down onto my floor. "I'm here now. Don't let the pretty face fool you, bitch, I'm still about that life."

Carissa stands up and says, "Mercedes, you got five seconds to get up out of my face. One..."

"Two, three, four, five," Mercedes responds counting down for her. "Now what, bitch?"

The next thing I know Carissa presses her brown fist into the center of Mercedes' yellow nose. Mercedes' eyes fly open, and blood flies out of her nostrils, and splatters over the blue t-shirt she's wearing. Mercedes counters her punch with a knee to Carissa's gut, sending Carissa descending to the floor.

Carissa holds her stomach. "I hate you, you red ugly bitch."

"Never ugly," Mercedes responds. "Just mad."

She looks like she's preparing to kick Carissa in the gut, when Carissa grabs her ankle and pulls her down to her level. Hair is flying everywhere and Mercedes has already come out of her shirt. All you see now is Mercedes' red titties, and her brown nipples in the air, and fists full of expensive weaves scattered on my living room floor. Carissa is tearing her apart.

My dogs are barking wildly in the room, and I yell at them to silence them up. They probably think somebody is hurting me, and I have no doubt they would rip into their flesh if I were being harmed.

The yelling and screaming has reached new heights and I'm getting irritated now. I live in an expensive neighborhood, and my sadity white and black neighbors don't take too kindly to explosive drama.

Any other time I would break the fight up, but I realized something recently. This fight between them is long overdue. So I sit on the sofa, grab the remote, and turn on the television. Thirty minutes pass before they eventually whine down, and I don't say a word until they are out of breath.

They look like they're playing some half-naked Twister game. Mercedes is naked from the waist up, and she's holding two fistfuls of Carissa's long black hair. Carissa has her arm around Mercedes' neck, and they are both breathing heavily.

"Are you two bitches done?" I ask.

"Tell her to get the fuck off of my neck," Mercedes says. "I can go another round I swear to God. You know I got stamina."

"Not until she gets off of my hair," Carissa replies. "I know I got potholes in my scalp now fucking with this bitch."

"How about both of ya'll let go at the same time," I suggest.

"I'm not getting up until this bitch let's my neck go," Mercedes promises. "We can be here all night, Yvette. I got a lot of shit on my heart I been trying to get off with this girl. For real I don't have nothing but time. Give me a few more seconds and we can box again."

When I see they are both determined not to give in, I walk to my room and open my door. My pitbulls come rushing into the living room, barking and acting wildly. They haven't been to the beauty dog salon so their nails are long and pointy. They hop all over them, and dig their dirty nails into the flesh of their skin.

Mercedes and Carissa separate, hop on the sofa and beg me to put them up. "Get your fucking dogs," Mercedes screams, pressing her naked titties against Carissa's chest. "Put them up."

"I'll put them up only if ya'll are done."

"We done," Carissa cries into Mercedes' shoulder. "Please put them up before I shoot 'em both."

"Bitch, don't play like that." I give her a serious look. "Some jokes get people killed around here." Carissa knows that I don't play when it comes to my animals. "Here boys." They follow me back to my room. I grab a t-shirt from my dresser, and close them inside the room. When I come back out into the living room, Carissa and Mercedes are sitting on opposite ends of my sofa.

"Now, can we talk about what's really going on?" I question them. I throw her the shirt and she slides it on and uses her old shirt to wipe her bloodied nose.

"I guess," Mercedes says throwing the rag in her lap and folding her arms over her breasts.

"I know that we don't like this situation with Karen, and the Black Water Klan. And we can all agree, after Persia has her baby something may have to give with them."

"But why does it have to give?" Carissa asks looking at us. "Why can't we just keep the peace? I mean I'm tired of all of the fighting, the murders and the crime. I can't take it anymore. You know sometimes I wish we never took Emerald City away from the boys. I wish we just walked away and let them have it all. We could've been happy. We could've had our families. Now we got all the money in the world, and we don't have nothing."

I feel like punching Carissa in the face after that comment. Emerald City holds our blood money. "We didn't do anything wrong by standing by Emerald City. We just fought for what belonged to us. Don't talk like that again around me, Carissa. You know how I feel about Emerald."

"Emerald is not a person, Yvette," Carissa continues grabbing the soiled rag out of Mercedes' lap to wipe her lip. "It's a trap. It's meant to hold us back from what we are really destined to do in life. I'm tired of it." She tossed the rag in her own lap.

"Then walk away," I tell her. "Because you sure didn't have no problem taking the money needed for Persia. Emerald City has its problems but it has always been good to us. Anyway, this isn't about Emerald. It's about you two, and your children. Mercedes, Persia was upset the other day. So what I want to know is this, is it true that you called Persia and cursed her out?"

"I can't believe ya'll would even think I'd call that little girl up to do some bamma shit like that," Mercedes says to me. "That's why I started spinning and wind-milling when I came in here. What the fuck I look like calling that baby chick? I knew that little girl when she couldn't even walk. When her clit wasn't developed. Give me credit for that, if you don't give me credit for nothing else."

"Then why would she tell me that?" Carissa yells. "You're supposed to be her aunt, Mercedes. Not her fucking enemy."

Mercedes frowns. "Look, the moment she fucked C, the aunt shit went out the window. I mean we can all agree that if she is carrying his baby, they can't be referred to as cousins anymore. That shit all the way weird and incestuous."

"You know what I mean."

"Yes I do," Mercedes continues. "But you have to understand something about Persia. Your daughter lies, and a lot too. So what I want to know is why are you sitting on the other end of this sofa acting like you don't know?"

"My daughter lies?" Carissa touches her chest.

"Carissa, you know that girl lies," I say. "And unlike Mercedes, I don't have direct ties to her so I can keep shit chief. She lies, and the sooner you realize that, the better you'll be able to deal with her. Otherwise she's going to get you into major trouble."

Carissa sits back into the sofa. "She doesn't necessarily lie, as much as she hides the truth."

"She lies," I repeat. "all the time too." I sit on the arm of my loveseat. "With that said, Mercedes, you can't antagonize her. Not only is it wrong because the girl is pregnant, but also because she's Carissa's daughter. Not one of us in this room wanted to see C and Persia fuck, but they have, and now we have a family crisis that must be dealt with.

"But I feel the need to remind you, that there is also another dark situation looming. If we aren't careful a war can ensue with the Black Water Klan, before we can get Persia out of there, and we don't need that right now. Who knows what lies Persia is telling Karen and them. So Mercedes, can I count on you to play fair with Persia? At least until we find out what we are going to do with the Klan?"

"I guess," she shrugs.

"Mercedes, please," I respond. "Although you still look young, you ain't no teenager no more. It's time to grow up and stop being immature."

Mercedes sighs. "I won't say nothing to her, just as long as she doesn't say nothing to me. I mean you got to forgive me if I'm not a fan of Persia's. She's the main reason me and my son don't have a bond anymore."

"That's a lie," I say.

"How you figure?"

"Because *you* are the reason ya'll don't have a bond anymore," Carissa interrupts. "Just like I'm the reason for the breakdown with my family, and with my girls." Carissa shakes her head. "I can't believe this shit. In the pursuit of money, we forgot what was really important. Family."

Mercedes shakes her head. "This shit is crazy. We are richer than we could have ever imagined, yet we're more fucked up in the head." She looks at Carissa and asks, "Would you give it all up if you could get Persia back? The money, the cars? Everything?"

Carissa looks at me, and then back at Mercedes. "Yes. I would. In a heartbeat." Carissa looks at me. "What about you, 'Vette?"

"You already know my answer. Without Emerald City, I'm dead. Anyway, ya'll so busy fighting that you have forgotten that I am engaged." I flash my twelve-carat diamond ring as a reminder. "But I haven't. We are supposed to be celebrating these days."

"I'm sorry, 'Vette," Mercedes says to me. "We been so involved in our own shit that we forgot about you. Are you excited? I mean ya'll are getting married in six-months right? I swear I'm looking forward to going to Hawaii for ya'll ceremony."

"I'm excited."

"But are you happy?" Carissa questions.

I don't know if I'm happy or not. I don't even love him. I do know that as it stands, I'm not doing anything else with the rest of my life right now, so I might as well give him a chance. He's a good businessman, he loves me to pieces and he isn't trying to change me. What more could a girl ask for?

"I'm happy."

"What about love," Carissa says. "Do you love him?"

Silence.

"Yvette, do you love him?" she repeats.

"I'll learn to love him. In time."

Judah and I are sitting in a dark romantic restaurant. We just finished eating and were waiting on the chocolate mousse that we are going to share. We just finished a bottle of wine. I notice that whenever we are together, I have to drink. The more I drink when I'm with him, the better I feel about our microwaved relationship.

"Were you ever in love before?" I ask him while looking into his eyes. He reaches for my hand across the table and I rub his fingers. "Because you don't talk a lot about your past."

"Yeah," he says. "I was in love before."

That hurts my feelings. I don't know what my problem is but there's something about being the first at everything that makes me feel better. It makes me feel safe. In the back of my mind I wonder if this is the kind of thing that he does all of the time. Meet some lonely girl, sweeps her off of her feet, and proposes. I hope he doesn't do some weird thing like leave me at the alter, and embarrass me in front of my friends.

"Did you ask her to marry you?"

"Yes I did. She said yes, but she didn't want to."

The mousse comes, but suddenly I don't want it anymore. "If you asked her to marry you, why didn't she? You're a total package. You are handsome, rich, awesome in the bedroom and you love dogs. Who wouldn't want to be Mrs. Judah Hassam?"

He gives me one of them half smiles that only rise on one side of his mouth. "She wasn't ready, Yvette," he picks his spoon up and stabs at the mousse. "I knew I wanted to marry her from the moment I saw her face. It was similar to what happened when I met you."

Uggh. What the fuck type shit is this?

"We had a happy life for a long time. I bought her the house of her dreams, gave her everything she could ever ask for, and asked her to marry me. She said no. When I told her if we weren't going to be serious that I was going to leave her alone, she gave in and said yes. But that was many, many years ago, 'Vette, and you don't have to worry about her anymore. She killed herself."

My lips push outward. "Killed herself?"

"Yes," he snaps. "Killed herself. As in took her own life. As in she not here anymore. As in she was a weak bitch."

Oh my God. Judah is crazy.

"Oh, I'm so sorry," I say sincerely. I touch the top of his hands. "Do you know why she committed suicide?"

"I don't know, and to tell you the truth, I'm happy about not knowing. Because there's nothing you can tell me that will make me understand why she chose such a weak move. Suicide is selfish when you're loved. I loved her harder than a man should ever love a woman, but I guess that wasn't good enough for her. I just wish I…"

I can't hear shit else Judah was spitting. Because while he was running his mouth, I was looking at Chris walk in with some beautiful girl with smooth brown skin, a size zero waist and a humungous ass.

My eyes move from her to Chris as they talk to the hostess. What the fuck is so funny? They look happy, and I feel like I'm carrying a fifty-pound moving baby in my stomach.

First let me talk about how good Chris looks. She was never big, but now she looks like she was in the gym hard since the last time I saw her. Her hair is cut into a curly bush, and she is dressed in some slick ass grey slacks, with a black short sleeve shirt. A pair of Gucci black shoes dress her feet.

The girl, who I have no doubt is Lace, is wearing a white dress, that hugs every curve of her body. They are smiling in each other's faces and they look like they don't have a care in the world. Until they see me.

They follow the hostess to their seats, but on the way stop at my table.

"Yvette," Chris says clearing her throat. "How are you?"

"Great." I try to smile but I know I'm frowning.

It's a good thing she stopped too. Because, if she would've walked past this table like she didn't know me, I would've put a hot slug in her back.

I'm so mad right now I can't see nothing but Chris' eyes. Who is she to be happy, and to go on with her life? Why isn't she at home, trying to find a thousand ways to get me back? She should be devastated that I didn't call her, after she told me she wasn't leaving Lace for me. But she isn't. She's happy. So what is going on?

"Baby, who is this?" Judah asks.

“Chris, This is my fiancé Judah,” I say.

Chris’ expression changes from confusion to sadness. She looks at me, and then at him. Finally I got the look I was going for. The look of pain and hurt. *Yeah, bitch. How does it feel?*

“Oh…well…congrats on your upcoming nuptials,” she gives Judah some dap. “This is my girlfriend Lace.”

“Hello, Yvette,” Lace smiles. Her teeth are so white they look unreal. “Chris has told me so many nice things about you. She says you are the strongest woman she has ever known. It’s nice to finally meet you.”

I can’t believe Chris said all of those nice things about me. Instead of being relieved that I’m still a topic of their relationship, it makes me sad even more. Chris is handling this break up with class, and I don’t know how to deal. I’m use to drama and pain.

“It’s nice to meet you too,” I shake Lace’s hand. It’s soft, and dainty, like a girl’s should be. Not small and hard like mine. I can tell she’s a kept woman. And if she marries Chris, I already know she’ll have a fairytale life.

“Enjoy the rest of your evening,” Chris says. “Bye, Yvette.”

“Who was—,”

“I’m ready to go home,” I say cutting Judah off. “Let’s go now.”

◄┈┈┈┈┈┈┈┈┈┈┈┈┈┈┈┈┈┈┈┈┈┈┈┈┈┈►

There is one way to get a female out of your mind, and that is to get some dick. So the moment we made it to Judah's place, I stripped him out of his pants, followed by his boxers. We were in the living room, and he is standing before me, naked from the waist down.

The funny thing is, even though his dick is limp, he is still packing. His rod is big, and smooth and has a large mushroom head, with a thick pulsating vein stretching down the middle.

I lie on the floor, face up, and open my mouth. "Come down here, Judah. I want to taste you."

He walks over to me and looks down at me. All I see is hairy dick and ass. "Are you okay?" he asks. "You haven't said a word since we left the restaurant. And when you do talk you want to suck my dick?"

I close my mouth and sigh. "Why are you complaining? You gonna come out good at the end of this."

"Do you want to talk, baby?"

"I want to suck your dick? Do you want me to get up?"

He shrugs and drops to his knees. I open my mouth and he placed the tip of his dick on my tongue like it's a thermometer. I want a mouth full of meat, and this romantic shit is not the mood I was aiming for. He's all nice and soft, and I'm irritated. I have to control this situation. I need my mind off of her. I want him to give me one of them rough face fucks that Thick use to give me, when he was all about himself, and getting his cum on.

I move my face to the side, and his dick falls out of my mouth and onto my chin. "Fuck my face, Judah. Fuck it rough too."

He scoots down, and leans over me. His dick hangs, and rubs against my stomach like the pendulum on a grandfather clock. "Baby, what the fuck is all of this shit about? Were you dealing with that chick at the restaurant or something? I saw how you looked at her, when she introduced her girlfriend, and it didn't feel right."

"Does it make a difference if I was?"

"Yes. I mean, you never told me you were into chicks."

I roll my eyes. "I'm not into chicks."

"Then what's going on?"

"Judah, I want to suck your dick, and you won't let me," I yell. "I have a problem with people not letting me do things that I want to do. Back in the day I was use to being denied, but I don't like being denied anymore. Now I know a rack of niggas who will give me what I want if I say the word. So what the fuck do you want to do?"

The look he gives me stops my heart, but he does what I'm asking for. His body lowers over my face and at first I'm scared. All I see is a hairy yellow chest, and a big dick coming at me quickly.

I open my mouth, and he stuffs his dick into my throat. His hairy stomach strokes against my nose, but I don't mind. I don't care about myself right now. I can taste his salty pre-cum trickle down my throat, before he takes the back of my head, and pumps in and out of my face like it's a pussy. My mouth is stuffed with vanilla colored dick, and I'm taking it like a pro.

When he's about to cum, Judah grabs my hair, and pushes deeper into my throat. I feel myself gagging on his meat stick but I don't tell him to stop. Tears puddle in my eyes, and roll back toward my ears. And, I think about the question Carissa asked me earlier about me being in love. No. I'm not in love.

"Open your mouth wider, bitch," Judah says waking me out of my thoughts. "I'ma give you what you want. A jaw full of nut."

I open my mouth so wide; my lips feel like they're going to split in the corners. I massage his meaty ass cheeks, until I can feel his vein pulsating against my tongue. When I feel his thick warm milk gush down my throat, I smile.

But you know what? After all of this face fucking, for some reason, I still can't get Chris, or that bitch she was with out of my mind. So that means one thing, Lace has to go. I don't want Chris to love anybody unless it's me.

Sorry, Chris. If I can't be happy, you can't either.

CHAPTER 11
CARISSA

I'm sitting on the living room floor, with my back leaned against the sofa. Between my thighs is a broken mirror, and the remnants of three lines of coke I snorted earlier. I'm feeling good. *Really good.* My left nostril tickles a little, and a small stream of blood oozes out of it, and falls onto my breastbone. I smear it away.

I know Yvette and Mercedes would never approve of my choice of high, so I do it alone, in the pleasure of my home. When my youngest daughter Treasure is with her friends, and I am depressed or lonely, this makes everything better. I'm not like some of them chicks who don't know how to stop, I just don't want too. That's why I miss Kenyetta so much. She was the one person who let me be me, and didn't try to change me. We use to snort bags of this shit together, and now she's dead. What a waste of a real bitch.

I'm feeling extra horny, so I'm about to play with my vibrator in my bedroom. I crawl on my hands and knees, and move toward my bedroom, until my doorbell rings.

"Who is it?" I call from the floor.

"It's me, ma. Open up."

My eyes pop open, and I jump off of the floor. Am I hearing things, or is that really Persia's voice? I push the mirror under the sofa with my big toe, and my foot accidently gets cut. Blood pours out of my toe, and I rub it against my cream carpet. Fuck it. I'll get a new rug. There is nothing more important than spending this time with my daughter.

I dust myself off and rush toward the door. Kind of paranoid, I look out of the peephole. I want to make sure she is not with one of them crazy Klan members. I see Persia standing on the other side wearing a cute baby blue velour jumpsuit. I quickly unlock and open the door. I pull her toward me in an embrace. "I can't believe you are here. You're home."

She looks me over. Suspiciously. "I do have to go back to the compound, ma. Don't get all extra sentimental and shit. We not like that." She looks inside. "Where Treasure?"

"She over Bria's house. Why?"

She walks inside, and I close and lock the door behind her. "No reason. Just asking I guess." She sits on the sofa. When I see the baggie of coke next to her foot, I walk over to her, and kick it under the sofa, before she sees it. "Why is blood on the floor, your foot and chest? It looks like a crime scene in here."

"I must've cut myself."

She shakes her head. "What's really wrong with you, ma? You still snorting that shit?"

My eyes widen. "What you talking about?" I frown.

"Stop the games, ma. Everybody knows that you and auntie Kenyetta was hoovering that shit. They called ya'll the Powder Puff Girls around Emerald City and everything. Use to fuck with me when I was at school too. I hated it." She looks like she wants to cry. "Anyway, it's cool though. The best thing about being a kid is that you eventually grow up, and move out."

I'm mortified. "I'm sorry they use to bother you at school, Persia. But I don't know what you're talking about. I don't snort nothing but air."

"Ma, you sound stupid."

"Persia, I'm just glad that you're here." I sit next to her. "So what's going on? I thought you weren't allowed off of the compound without authorization."

"That rule only applies if you aren't fucking the leader's son," she says smacking her lips.

My heart breaks. "Are you telling me that you are having sex while you're pregnant? Persia, you gotta slow down. You can hurt the baby."

She giggles. "Ma, just because I'm baking a bun, don't mean I can't have a little fun. If anything I'm hornier now, since I'm pregnant. Don't worry though, I ain't do nothing yet. It would be nice to be with my child's father but aunt Mercedes fucked that up for me and C."

"Persia," I yell. "What is wrong with you these days? Why do you talk to me like I'm not your mother?"

"You need only look at yourself to answer that question. Why should I give you respect, when none is given? You fucked me and Treasure up in the head, ma. Real good too. I don't know why you think you get to have the dream children because of it."

She crushed me with one swipe of her tongue.

"Did you talk to aunt Mercedes?"

"Yes I did."

"Did you curse her out?" she grins, rubbing her pregnant belly. "For disrespecting me, and your future grandbaby."

"Something like that," I respond.

"I should've known that you would be too weak to do what should've been done." She shakes her head. "You have allowed Mercedes to run everything you do. Even this beef with the Black Water Klan started over some girl that *Mercedes'* son was fucking. This is all her fault, and I wish you could just see that, ma."

"So now he's Mercedes' son? I thought you referred to him as The Great C."

"You know what I mean." She pouts. "Had C not been so jealous that Tamir had fucked his girl, the war would not have started with ya'll and them. It seems like Mercedes and her family is not happy unless they're getting what *they* want. Everything is all about *them*. I'm just sorry that you aren't smart enough to see it."

"Persia, let's focus on us," I say. "Leave Mercedes out of it. You're not going to be here too long, and I want us to spend this time together."

Suddenly Persia breaks out crying. My heart tugs when I see her tears fall on her sweat suit and make dark raindrops on her belly. What a bitch I am. I'm always talking about Mercedes hurting my daughter's feelings, and here I am doing the same thing. So I move closer to her, pull her into my arms and rock her softly. How I use to do when she was a baby. A little baby, smelling of baby powder and lotion.

She cries into my chest and her pregnant belly presses against mine. "Persia, please don't cry. I didn't mean to yell at you. I really didn't. I just don't want you to think so long and hard about Mercedes. Everything will be okay, I promise."

"But it's mostly her fault that I ran away, mommy. All of this is her fault." She's crying so hard now that she's stuttering. "I-I felt like you weren't t-taking my side," she continues. "I-I love you, mommy. I really do. B-but if you are going to keep Mercedes in your life, I guess I'll have to move on with my new family, and I'll never see you again. At least I know they love me."

"Persia, that isn't a family over there. You can't trust them people. I know I haven't been the best mother in the world, but I love you and Treasure with all of my heart. I need you to understand that."

When her phone dings, she sits up straight. Amazingly, the crying stops like someone turned off a water faucet. She wipes the tears from her face like it was nothing to begin with, and removes the cell phone from her purse. It's a text message, and from where I sit I can read it.

'BWK BULLETIN. Please report to the compound immediately. There is an emergency within the family.'

Persia stuffs the phone into her purse and hops up. "I have to go, ma."

I stand up too. "Is everything okay? Do you need me to come with you?"

"No, but I need you to remember what I said. If you want a relationship with me, you gotta choose me over Mercedes. I'm sorry, ma, but I just don't feel safe around her anymore. And if I can't feel safe, I can't be around you. Bye."

CHAPTER 12
MERCEDES

I'm in Bells and Diamonds, a full service wedding planning company with Carissa. I'm looking at a model wearing one of the 'Matron Of Honor' dresses Yvette chose for me. I don't know why, but for some reason I hate everything about it. I don't know if it's because the model's body is frumpy, or if it is the design itself. It may even be because since we first got here Carissa, has been yapping my head off non-stop about Persia.

"You should've heard her," Carissa says sitting next to me. "She said if I don't stop dealing with you, then we won't have a relationship."

I turn around to face her, and I can tell that this bitch is really serious. We have been friends forever. We've gone through things that most friends will never have to deal with in their lifetime. Carissa is my sister, and as much as we fight I love her. Yet she's coming at me with this shit.

"Carissa, are you asking for permission not to be my friend?"

"What?" she giggles. "Of course not."

"Then what are you saying?"

"I don't know what I'm saying," she says out of breath. "I just want my daughter to be happy. I want us all to get along, if nothing else for the baby."

"Can you try the other dress on please, I don't like that one," I tell the model.

"What's wrong with it?" the model asks me.

This chick got me confused with one of her little friends. "Bitch, take the fucking dress off and put on another one."

When she leaves I focus on Carissa. "I'm not going to lie, with everything you throwing at me, Carissa, I'm starting to get a headache. We'll talk about Persia later."

She sighs. "Okay." She looks at the bride's maid dresses in front of her. "Why didn't Yvette ask me to be the Matron of Honor? Why I gotta stand next to Judah's cousins and shit? She don't even know them like that?"

"Do you really have to ask me why I'm the Matron of Honor? I mean, it ain't like you not in the wedding."

"I'm asking. Why she pick you and not me?"

"First off you should be asking her. Second of all don't act like you not familiar with the hierarchy of our friendship. It has always been me and Yvette and you and Kenyetta."

"I know, but Kenyetta is gone," Carissa replies. "And now I feel like I don't have anybody to rap to about my problems. I mean you got Yvette and Toi, but it seems like nobody wants to be around me. It's like if I'm not talking shop, ya'll don't want to hang out."

"That's not true."

"So you didn't go over Yvette's house the other day to have dinner with her and Judah?"

I clear my throat. "Yes but—"

"She didn't say shit to me about it, Mercedes. I ain't been over her house since I fought you."

"You mean since I fought your ass."

"We both fought each other," Carissa replies rolling her eyes. "As a matter of fact, I didn't hear anything about the dinner until she told me how much fun ya'll had. It's like I'm not a part of the clique anymore."

"That's not true," I say. "You know, 'Vette loves you very much and I do too. She wants you around."

Oh my God she's getting on my fucking nerves with all this sentimental shit. She's so whack sometimes. If she didn't want you to come, so what?

"But it's how I feel, Mercedes. Don't you see, I'm calling out for help right now? I feel alone."

I sigh. Truth is I do hate being with Carissa sometimes. She's whiny, she's annoying and I have a feeling she's still on coke. She thinks somebody stupid, but I'm far from it. Me and 'Vette talked about it while we were cooking dinner, before Judah came over the other day. I'm not with the coke shit. I mean, why would I want to ride with someone who moves like that in the world? I love her, but I prefer to do it from a far.

I'm about to respond to Carissa, when I receive a text message. I remove my phone from my purse. The text is from Yvette.

Yvette: 'What about that thing I needed done?'

Me: 'It's complete.'

Yvette: 'That's Y I luv u.'

Me: 'Tell me somethin' I don't know.'

When I'm done with her, I throw my phone back in my purse and address Carissa. "Carissa, you know you family, and that will never change. But if you want to be a part of us, I mean really a part of us, you have to take initiative. Yvette is always inviting herself over my house, and I do the same thing to her. But people get tired of inviting you places, only for you to cancel. If we ain't going to a party, you not with it, and that's not right. So the invitations stopped coming to you. Friendship is two sided, or in this instance, three sided. We grown women now. We don't have our boyfriends to force us together to sit on the stoop in front of Unit C anymore. We bosses, and if you want to be loved, you have to give love in return."

She gets quiet but I tune her out anyway. Why? Because some fine ass dude walks up to me. He has to be about 6'4, and super attractive, with skin the color of a Werther's Original caramel candy. He was wearing a navy blue designer suit, and I figured he was the owner of the store.

"Hi, I understand you want to see some more dresses?" he asks me.

"Yeah, but I don't think you'll look good modeling them for me," I say to him, flirting a little. "I don't think they're your style."

"You right about that," he says in his deep voice. "I wouldn't do them justice, but I bet you'll look sexy in them. Do you know which one you want to see?"

"It doesn't matter, you can bring me any one of them. My friend picked them out, and they have all been a mess anyway."

"Then go naked."

My mouth hangs open, until Carissa sticks her nasty finger into it, which rubs against my tongue. I close my mouth, and she snatches her finger out.

"Ugh, why would you put your nasty finger into my mouth?" I wipe my lips.

"Because you acting like you want him to stick his dick in there instead," Carissa says.

She's playing me super hard now in front of this nigga, and I'm trying to maintain my cool. "Carissa, why don't you go on over there, and see what beastly dresses Yvette picked out for you. I'm busy over here."

She rolls her eyes, but thank God she leaves.

"What's your name?" I ask him.

"Lloyd," he smiles.

I swear my pussy is thumping like a drum right now. *Ba-rum-pa-pum-pum.*

"Lloyd, what are you doing in here? You gonna get me fired," the girl who was modeling the dresses says to him.

"You don't work here?" I ask frowning.

I hold my purse closely to me, preparing to shoot to kill if this is a set up. I'm thinking between my legs instead of remembering I'm worth a lot of money. There are a lot of jealous niggas in the world who want me dead. Carissa is already back next to me gripping her purse too.

"No I don't work here," he smiles again. "But I saw you over here and figured I don't have nothing to lose. I decided to come over here and kick it with you."

"You playing yourself," the model says to him. "You don't have a job, you don't have a car, and our mother still spoils you, plus you wearing daddy's clothes. This woman is a boss, and she don't have time for none of that shit."

"Excuse me, but are you speaking for me?" I ask her.

She looks embarrassed. "No, I just didn't want my brother over here bothering you that's all."

"The only person that's bothering me is you. So how 'bout you get lost so I can kick it with your brother for a second, cool?"

She rolls her eyes and walks away.

"Wow, nobody has ever spoken to my sister like that before," he says with a smile. "I like you already."

"Lloyd, let's cut to the chase I got things to do today. I'm not looking for love, I've done that already and it didn't work. I'm about having a good time, and I'm about someone who makes it their job to put a smile on my face. You want the job?"

"I don't see why not."

"Well let's exchange numbers and go from there," I say.

I feel so liberated with my new attitude. I'm not interested in meeting another Cameron or Derrick. I just want to kick it with someone who looks as sexy as I do, with no strings attached.

We exchanged numbers, he asked for a hug, which I thought was lame, and I said no.

"You gonna be mine," he tells me.

"Slow down, Lloyd," I say with my hand out. "One step at a time."

When he leaves the store, I text Toi.

Me: 'Meet me at Bells & Diamonds.'

Toi: 'I'm on my way. I'm kind of hungry though.'Me: 'Me too.'

Although Yvette almost messed my friendship up with Toi, she was right about one thing, Toi was a real bitch and was able to move past me pulling a gun on her. Her only request was that I keep her separated from Yvette, and I was cool with that. Besides, I'm sure Yvette and Carissa will have friends in the future that I won't like. I guess when Kenyetta died, so did the idea of the foursome-friendship circle I was accustomed too.

Fifteen minutes later Toi walks through the door. She looks so pretty in her peach dress and yellow Manolo Blahnik sandals. We hug and she says,

“Ready to hit the town? I'm trying to go down to the National Harbor."

"Yes, but let me say bye to Carissa first." I walk over to Carissa and say, "I'm about to head out. I'll get up with you later okay?"

She looks over my shoulder. "Why didn't Toi say hi?”

"Not for nothing, but after the way Yvette treated her, I think it isn’t smart to mix the cliques.”

“But what about Persia? I thought we were going to talk more about that."

I sigh. “Carissa, Persia is your problem like C is mine. If you believe that the best thing for your relationship is to sever our friendship, that will hurt my feelings, a lot, but I’ll understand and won’t try to stop you."

I’m lying. If she does that shit she is as good as dead to me.

“Mercedes, I’m asking you to stay with me tonight,” she says. “Don’t go. I need you.”

“You can’t be serious, Carissa. Me and Toi were about to get something to eat.”

She rolls her eyes. “So you choosing her over me? Somebody you’ve known most of your life?” I don’t respond. “Mercedes, please hang out with me tonight.”

“What is this really about?” I ask. “Are you testing me?”

She frowns. “You know what, it don’t even matter, Mercedes. One day you gonna want me to remember you, and I’m going to think about this shit.”

As she walks away I hear her say. “Persia was right, she is selfish.”

Now I’m mad. I knew she was testing me, because of that bitch she gave birth to. I’m more determined than ever to get Monie right to steal C’s heart. Now I’m making it extra personal.

CHAPTER 13
KAREN

Karen is in the basement in the main building of the BWK headquarters. She's staring at a sea of her people. They are sitting in metal black chairs, and watching her as she stands next to the podium. Karen is wearing a black dress suit, with extra-thick shoulder pads, and her stare is intense. To Karen's right is her son Oscar, and to her left are Roman and Lance.

Many members in the audience try their best to maintain their calmness. It's difficult, because they have no idea of what could have happened to cause this emergency meeting.

"Before Black Water was murdered some years back we were strong," Karen begins speaking to the Klan. "When he died we were all worried, and concerned that we wouldn't be able to provide for ourselves. Later, Tamir came up with an idea that put us back on top. We submerged ourselves into the drug industry, and we were able to support our family. We bought these buildings, we prospered and we were able to protect our beliefs. When Tamir died we were back at square one, but there was one

thing they couldn't take from us this time, our strength and our resolve. No matter what happened we had our anonymity, and the faithfulness we pledged to the Klan."

Karen eyeballed one of the younger teenagers, who were promised to Lance for next year. Hives popped up on her brown cheeks when Karen looked at her, and she scratched into her skin.

"Do you know what anonymity means, Denise?" Karen questions the beautiful teenager.

"Yes, my Lord."

"What does it mean?" Karen persists.

"It means to have no individuality outside of the Klan. It means that we are not ourselves individuals, but we are one."

"Correct," Karen agrees. She observes another young girl. Her light skin is riddled with pimples. "What about you, Stephanie? Do you know what faithfulness means?"

"Yes, my Lord," the girl responds trembling.

"Explain."

She clears her throat. "It means to be loyal, consistent and never wavering. It's the Black Water Klan or death."

"Correct," Karen nods. "And since it seems true, that all are aware of what we stand for, can someone please tell me why there is a plague of deceit amongst us?"

"I don't know what you mean, my Lord," Denise responds, since Karen is looking at her again. "I have never been deceitful in any way."

"Well maybe Gia can explain this to me," Karen frowns after spotting her in the crowd. "Gia, come up here and face your family."

Gia's stands up from her seat. She's a beautiful girl with skin the color of wet sand. Her nine-month pregnant belly leads the way toward the front. Her teeth rattle. The tension in the room had now risen higher than a 450-degree oven. Gia stood next to Karen. She's trembling.

"Gia, did you or did you not take Tamir as your husband, before he died?" Karen asks.

"I did, my Lord."

"And do you bear his child in your womb?"

"I do, my Lord."

"Then tell me why are you harboring a disease that has the power to snuff out our entire family?"

Gia cried uncontrollably. "I don't know, my Lord. I have been faithful to Tamir since the day he took me as his wife. I never even looked at the other men here, even when they optioned me after Tamir was murdered. I cooked for him. I cleaned for him, and I never disrespected him."

"Then how could this be?"

Gia swallowed. "I don't know, my Lord. Maybe he gave me HIV."

The entire room gasped until Karen raised her tiny hand to silence them all.

"Are you telling me that Tamir infected you with this disease?" Karen frowned.

"Yes, my Lord," Gia persisted. "Prior to Tamir I had never been with another man. I was a virgin.

The only person my mother use to allow over my house was Tamir."

"Lies," someone yelled.

"This bitch needs to be dealt with now," demanded another. "She could have infected all of the men."

Karen raised her hand again. "Silence." When the room was quiet she said, "I need to see a show of hands of everyone who has been with Tamir."

Although many hands went into the air, including Gia's, Karen chose to hide the fact that she herself had been with him. It was a night to remember.

Tamir had chosen Karen, Gia, Energy and finally his own mother, for an orgy some days before he was murdered. But, the only one who was alive to know that Karen had also slept with Tamir was Gia, since everyone else had been killed. Karen was certain that Gia wouldn't say a thing, and she was right.

When Karen saw the most beautiful women in the Klan raise their hands she sighed. She also looked upon Persia, who surprisingly enough, hadn't raised her hand. Karen was somewhat relieved because at least Oscar's future wife should be clean, in the event Tamir was infected.

"You can put your hands down," Karen said. "Roman, go get the guest of honor."

Roman walked to a closed door off of the basement, and brought out a white man. The white man walked toward the front. "Stand next to me," Karen ordered him. The man did. "This is doctor Hough-

ton," Karen told the members. "And he's going to examine everyone in here today. Whoever hosts the HIV disease will be identified, and I do mean everybody."

CHAPTER 14
YVETTE

I'm pulling up on my block after meeting with Judah. He's so excited about the wedding, but I'm just not feeling it anymore. The fucked up part is I don't have a choice. If I don't marry Judah, I could possibly ruin our business relationship too. He supplies Emerald and Camelot, so he has me. I must marry a man I don't love or like.

When I park my Range in front of my house, I'm immediately worried. My dogs are usually at the gate, in my front yard, waiting on my arrival. The only time they weren't was a year ago. I had left them out longer than I should have, and they had gotten out and scared the shit out of Ms. Lucy, and her two-year-old grandson, while they were walking to the park on day. My dogs are loving, but nobody cares when the breed of dogs you've chosen starts with Pit.

When I ease out of my car, and walk to the back of the house, I see my door hanging wide open. I slowly take my gun out of my purse, and toss my purse on the ground. Whoever is in my house is about to die.

I carefully step onto the first wooden stair, and it creaks. I aim into the house and yell, "Whoever is inside of my crib, I'm giving you five seconds to get the fuck up out my house, before I light this bitch up."

Silence.

"Do you hear me?"

"Come inside, Yvette. I've been waiting on you."

The gun hangs lower in my hand, when I hear her voice. I amble inside, and into the kitchen. Chris is sitting at the kitchen table. Two wine glasses sit in front of her; one filled with Merlot and the other is empty. Her light skin is red, and she looks like she may have been crying.

"What are you doing here?" I ask, walking inside slowly. "And how did you get in here?"

She looks up at me. Her eyes are bloodshot red. "I'd think you'd be happy to see me. Since you went through so much trouble to get me here."

"How did you get in my house?" I repeat.

"I took the key from the inside of Dobby's collar. You really should find another place to hide your spare key. If I got it off of him somebody else could have too."

"Naw, that's the best place. How many people could take anything off of Dobby's collar that he doesn't know?"

"None," she says.

I look toward the living room. It's really quiet. "Where are my dogs now?"

"In your room."

"Dobby…Rico," I yell. They bark loudly in response to my voice.

"Your dogs are okay, Yvette. You know that."

Relieved, I stuff my .45 into the back of my jeans. "Well, what's up?"

I lean my back against the refrigerator, and stare at her. Although she looks angry, I forget how good it feels to have her here. To have her home. Before it was over between us, we were happy. Well, I was happy. I made breakfast for her most mornings, and she prepared dinner at night. And then things changed. She wanted more of my time, which I couldn't provide. I fought so hard for Emerald City, that I put nothing before it, even her. What a mistake.

She pours me a glass of wine, and slides it in my direction across the table. "Drink with me," she says.

I stand up, walk toward her and reach for the glass. But her hand slaps across my wrist like a handcuff. The glass tumbles out of my hand, and crashes against the floor. Wine splashes everywhere, including my pants. She looks like she wants to kill me. I reach for my gun, but she's quicker than me and snatches it out of my jeans.

She cocks it, aims at me and says, "Sit down, Yvette."

"Chris, you're making me mad."

"Fuck your feelings," she screams. "Now sit down."

"What are you gonna, do shoot me?"

She fires into the floor next to where I stand. The smell of the gunpowder causes my adrenaline to course through my body. My dogs bark wildly in the background. I pull out a chair, take a seat, and wait nervously for my fate.

"My dogs aren't gonna stop barking," I tell her. "Let me go calm them down, before somebody calls the police."

"Be quiet, Dobby and Rico," she shouts. "Now!"

They quiet immediately. I hate my dogs so much right now. I forget that she knows them, and they respect her. That's the only way she was able to take the key from around Dobby's neck, without getting bitten.

"What's going on, Chris?"

I try not to look into the barrel of my own gun, but I can't help it. I pulled that weapon on hundreds of people in my lifetime, and now I finally understand how it feels to have it pulled on me. I gotta say, it's not a good feeling.

"Are you happy?" Chris asks. She walks up to me and runs the barrel of the gun alongside my temple. The barrel burns and I squint. "Did you accomplish what you set out too?"

"I don't know what you're—," My statement is cut when she fires another bullet into the wall. It misses my ear by inches.

"I've been drinking all day, Yvette," she says to me. "No water, straight alcohol, all day long. And on top of that, I'm having one of the worst days of my life. I can't even remember having a day more fucked up than this. So please don't belittle me by playing mind games. I can't be held responsible for what I might do to you. Now I asked you a question and I want an answer."

"No," I say.

She walks toward the stove and leans against it. "No what?" My gun is still aimed at me.

"No I'm not happy." My head drops and I clutch my hands in front of me on the table. "I haven't been happy for quite some time now, Chris. Is that what you want to hear?"

"Is it the truth?"

"Yes, it is."

She walks up to the table, and lowers the gun. "She was innocent, Yvette. Lace's only crime was saying yes to being my wife. She was murdered in her car, while talking to me on the phone." She looks at the floor. "Why would you take her from me? And why would you do it like that?"

"Because I didn't want her to love you."

"But why," she yells waving the gun wildly. "You made it clear that you couldn't be with me. Remember, every time I wanted to spend time with you, you told me you had an operation to run. Not only that you told me I couldn't live without you, but guess what, I did. So why won't you let me go?" She asks. "Why would you do something so cold and take an innocent person's life?"

"I can't be alone," I say.

"Alone? What about that nigga I saw you with at the restaurant," she says talking with the gun. "You told me you was getting married and everything, and I thought you was happy!"

"I'm not."

"Then what the fuck do you want from me?" she screams.

"I want you to love me, even if I can't love you back," I say.

"Oh my God, I can't believe this shit is happening to me. The only thing I did was try to love you, Yvette. That was my only crime. You want it all."

"I want everything," I say.

She lowers her head, and shakes it slowly from left to right. "She was loved, Yvette. Lace was the mother of a beautiful four year old little girl, and you took her away. Snuffed her out like she never existed."

My heart stops. "What…what do you mean she has a daughter? I thought she was gay."

"So because she's gay she can't have kids?"

My heart is beating fast and I'm hyperventilating.

"You didn't know did you," Chris asks, looking into my eyes. "You see what happens when you move with a jealous heart? You gonna pay for this shit. Remember what you told me some time back?"

"No," I say.

I'm still trying to wrap my mind around what I did. When I ordered Mercedes to put someone onto Lace, to have her killed, I assumed that because

Lace was gay, that she didn't have any kids. I have killed many people in my lifetime, some were mothers, but I never deliberately killed a square that didn't deserve it before now.

The sad part is that I just finished telling Mercedes that she was going to pay for Derrick's death, because Lil C loved him. And now I was learning that I had done the same thing.

"You told me that when you kill someone who's loved, it always comes back on you in some kind of way. My question is, what you think you will pay for this, 'Vette?"

"Chris, I'm sorry. I didn't—,"

"Care?" She pauses. "Is that what you were going to say?"

"No, I was going to say I didn't know. I saw you with her at the restaurant and flipped out. I would've never given the order had I known she had a child. I didn't stop to think what it would mean if I had Lace killed. I…I mean…is the child's father in the picture?"

"No," she says flatly. "But even if he was, you can't replace a mother's love, you know that, 'Vette. I mean, how many times have you told me that your mother's absence fucked with your head? And, that because she was gone you allowed yourself to be abused and treated badly by men? Now you put the same shit on an innocent kid."

"You don't know what the fuck you talking—,"

"Shut the fuck up, bitch," Chris yells at me. "Just shut the fuck up, I'm talking now. I'm tired of hearing your fucking voice! You nothing but the devil!"

Since the first day I met Chris, when she helped me carry my addicted mother to a car after she fell down the steps, she has never called me out of my name until now. And when I look into her eyes I can tell she's done with me. I think that hurts more than anything.

"You not use to a nigga treating you with love and respect, and I finally get it. So you have officially lost my respect, and you have lost my love."

I feel like she's stabbing me repeatedly in the heart.

"I'm done with you, Yvette," she yells, "I wish I never met you."

"Chris, I'm sorry. I'm so sorry."

She laughs at me. "That's not gonna be good enough this time. Stay right there," she tells me waving the gun. "Or I'll blow your head off of your shoulders."

She walks deeper into my house. I can't see what she's doing but I hear my bedroom door open. "How you doin' boys?" she says to my dogs. "I miss ya'll."

The next thing I hear stops my heart. One shot rings out, followed by the cry of one of my dogs. I'm on my feet and rushing to the back, before I hear another shot and another yelp. When I push open my bedroom door, I see my two Pitbulls lying on the floor in their own blood.

I rush up to her, and hit her in the back. "I hate you," I scream. "I fucking hate you!"

I try to take my gun back but she raises it into the air, and unloads the remaining bullets into the ceiling fan. When she's done she drops the gun on the floor and walks out of my room.

I run behind her and hit her on the back with heavy fists. Although she jerks forward with every blow, she doesn't fall. Chris continues to walk to the back door, coolly, and when she reaches it I push her out.

She turns around and faces me. "I bet that hurt didn't it," she smirks. "But that's only a small tidbit of what's coming for you. You took my kindness as a weakness, Yvette. Big mistake. Now you got another enemy. I shared your bed, and I know you, but you have no idea what I'm capable of."

CHAPTER 15
MERCEDES

I'm on my king sized bed. Lloyd's warm leg is draped over mine, as he's holding me from behind. Every so often I wiggle my ass against his dick, and it stiffens just the way I like it.

I know my friends won't approve of my arrangement with Lloyd, but I don't care because it works for me. After Cameron broke my heart, by choosing money over me, and after Derrick chose a bottom bitch over the love of his wife, I decided that whatever attention I received from a man, I would buy.

"What do you want, Mercedes, "Lloyd's deep voice calls out to me from behind. He pulls me closer to him. "You're the most beautiful woman I've ever met in my life, but you seem sad. Unfulfilled."

I sigh. Lloyd's only problem is that he talks too much. He's too corny at times. I wish he had an off button. "Why do you say that?"

"Because you deserve more than what you're asking of me," he says.

I turn around and look into his eyes. Damn this man is fine. "What do you mean I deserve more?

You're going to give me everything I desire, without the hang-ups of love and marriage. If anything, this arrangement will allow me to function, and to take care of the things I couldn't before, because some nigga was inside my head. Inside my heart and mind."

"I get that, Mercedes, but I feel bad that you're giving me money, just to sleep in your bed. I'll do this shit for free."

"But, I don't want you to do it for free," I tell him, rubbing his cheek. "I want you to treat this as a job. I've hired you, and you are at work. This way I'm buying your services, as opposed to hoping or wishing that you'd do what I want."

"But I'm sure I can learn to love you," he says.

I sit up in the bed, and look down at him. "Stand up, Lloyd."

"I thought we were about to take a nap."

"I said, stand up."

He gets out of the bed, and it squeaks. I need a new mattress. Everybody from Cameron to Derrick has been on this bitch. It's time to start anew.

Lloyd walks over to my side of the bed, and stands before me. "Pull down your pajama pants."

"Mercedes, you can't be—"

"I really hate to repeat myself," I tell him. "So I feel the need to remind you that you are at work. Now if I have to say it again, I want you out of my condo." He removes his blue Polo pajamas, which I bought by the way.

"Now what?"

"Dance for me." He looks like he's about to protest, but I guess he remembered what I said so he wiggles his waist, and I have to admit he looks stupid. I remind myself that it's not about what he's doing, it's about him doing what I say.

"Like this?"

"Yes, now move your waist harder, and faster." He moves his waist into large circles, and before I know it, his dick wakes up, and sticks out at me. "I see you're hard."

"That's because I'm looking into your eyes," he says. "And it's obvious that for whatever reason, this turns you on. And when you're turned on, I am too."

"Good, because I want you to beat your dick in front of me."

He stops dancing and leans in. "Are you serious?"

I look at him. The next time he questions me, he's fired.

He takes his dick into the palm of his hand, and strokes it back and forth. His honey brown stick lengthens, and reddens a little. For the first minute or so he's faking, and I can tell he doesn't really want to do it. But when I lean back on the bed, spread my legs, and open my pink juicy pussy, he gets into the groove.

"I like that, Lloyd," I tell him fingering myself back and forth. "I like how you look beating that stick."

"You gonna taste it for me?" he asks.

I frown at him. "This is my show not yours. If you want to boss me around feel free to make your purchase. But, I must admit, I'm not as cheap as you are. My price is kinda steep, and you could never afford me."

I can tell his feelings are hurt, but a minute later he looks like he forgets, when I get so wet, my oil rolls out of my hole, and falls onto the sheet beneath me. I'm feeling so good watching this man do everything I ask, that before I know it, I cum all over my fingers.

"Mmmmmm," I moan reaching my place. "That was sweet."

The moment I say that, cum shoots out of his dick, and splashes against my inner thigh. "Oh my, Gawd," he says. "I never did no shit like that before."

"Well you did a good job for your first time. So what do you notice about me?"

"I notice that you're beautiful."

"Save the melodramatics for the chicken heads you roll with," I say seriously. "I'm asking you what do you notice about me?"

"You seem satisfied."

"Exactly," I grin. "Because I got what I wanted, and what I wanted was for you to be at my beckon call. I don't want love, nor do I need it, Lloyd. I will never be your housewife, and I will never love you back if you fall for me. I advie you not to do it. So I'm asking if you think you can handle this, because it's all I have left?"

He grabs a few tissues from the box on my end table. He wipes the cum off my inner thigh, and then cleans his dick. "It's not what I had in mind when I met you," he throws the soiled tissue in the trash by the bed, "but if that's the only way I can have you, I guess I'm going along for the ride."

"Good, because I'll buy you anything you desire. You can move into my home tomorrow, and tend to my every need. If there's a bill in your name, I'll pay for it. If there's a situation that needs handled in your life, tell your mama and I'll care for it. I don't want you stressed about anything."

"Why?" he asks in a low voice.

"Because your one and only job in life will be me. I know it's selfish, but its what I want, and I get what I want."

"Okay," he says in a low voice.

I bet he never expected this shit when he pulled up on me at the wedding planners. "But, there's a downside in fucking with me, Lloyd. By agreeing to play on my terms, you're essentially pledging your loyalty to me. And I take loyalty very seriously."

"So do I."

"Good, because if you break the agreement, I will have you killed, Lloyd, and I'll buy another one who looks better than you the next week."

CHAPTER 16

KAREN

The sun shined brightly outside, and every member of the Black Water Klan was assembled quietly, and standing in front of the buildings. Karen stood in front of them holding a brown clipboard in her hand. A yellow number two pencil, with a sharp point, lay clenched between her white teeth. And the red book is stuffed under her arm.

Rumors circled the compound all day, as members tried to determine what the purpose of today's meeting meant for their family.

On the sidewalk were two white vans, with drivers waiting inside with the engines running. Something definitely was going to happen today, but what?

"If I call your name and follow it with the letter B, you must stand to my left," Karen spoke. "If I call your name and follow it with the letter A, you must stand to my right. Are there any questions?"

"No, my Lord," they all respond.

When one of the members approach Karen to whisper in her ear, the roll call is momentarily placed on hold.

In the far back of the crowd stood Persia, and Gia, who also wondered about today's fate.

"What do you think she is going to do?" Persia whispered to Gia. "When she finds out who else is HIV positive? I'm like real scared."

"I don't know," Gia said softly, holding Persia's hand. The two weren't best friends, but since they were close in age and both pregnant, they formed a light bond. "I gotta feeling it won't be nice. I guess it depends on what is in that book she always carries around. She opens it for all of her answers."

"You know what's in it?"

"Nope," Gia said.

Persia looks at Gia's face. The sun has turned her eyes into light brown crystals. "You scared?" Persia asked her.

"I ain't never been more scared in all my life," she exhaled. "But I was telling the truth, I ain't never been with anybody but Tamir. So if I got the disease, he had to give it to me. Do you think she'll kill me, since I'm pregnant with his baby?"

"I don't know," Persia shrugged. "I don't know if she care about no babies, more than she cares about the disease." Persia shakes her head. "I can't believe I almost fucked him, but on the night I was supposed to go into his room, he had somebody else in there already. I think it was his mother."

Gia likes Persia, but she's not sure if she can trust her enough to tell her that she was in the room that night, along with Karen.

"If I die, can you get in contact with my mother?" Gia asked.

Persia frowned and released her hand. "What I wanna do that for?"

"Because when I left home, to move here with Tamir, I never got to tell my mother that I loved her. She was good to me, Persia. Real good, and I miss her so much. But, I wanted to be with Tamir, and I was afraid that she would not approve of me being pregnant. Now I miss her terribly."

Persia thought she sounded dumb. Who misses their mother? "Humph, she must've been a real gem," Persia said jealously.

"She is, do you got a mother?"

Persia thought about Carissa and grew angry. Most of Persia's life, Carissa was present but preoccupied. If Carissa wasn't throwing her to a babysitter, she was throwing her to one of Mercedes' babysitters. Persia spent most of her life growing up with C, Chante, Treasure and random neighborhood kids. And, when Carissa was home, and Persia tried to spend time with Carissa, Carissa was never mentally available. The final straw came when Persia was twelve years old, and Carissa forgot her birthday. That was the day hate began to brew in Persia's heart for her mother. What kind of woman would forget her own daughter's birthday?

The thing was, Lavelle, her father, didn't forget. Although Carissa kicked him out of the house, he sneaked inside her home, when Carissa was with the Pitbulls, and brought Persia a beautiful pink birth-

day cake and her first designer purse. Persia loved her father deeper that day, and she never forgave her mother.

To this day, Carissa was unaware that she failed to celebrate one of her daughter's birthdays. She and Lavelle had spent so much energy fighting, that time just got away from her. Carissa tried to make up for her absences by spoiling her daughters but that only made matters worse. Persia wanted love, and Carissa failed to deliver. Now, Persia was resentful, angry and out for blood.

"I got a mother," Persia responded, answering Gia's question. "But it don't make me no difference. She be dead to me in my head anyway."

"That's sad. Cause if you got a chance to be with your family you should really do it," Gia begged. "While you still can."

"Why I want to do that for?"

"Because real family, the ones who got your flesh and blood, will always be in your corner," Gia responded.

"But this is our family now," Persia said. "You need to forget the past, Gia. It might get you into more trouble."

"This is not a real family," Gia frowned. She looked up front to be sure Karen was still busy with one of the members. She was. "They will take you for all they can, and throw you away. I'm talking about your body, your money and your spirit. Persia, if you got a chance to go be with your mother, you should run now. It may be too late for me."

"I will never turn my back on the Klan," Persia said getting a little louder. "And you shouldn't either, traitor." She pointed at Gia and her index finger stabbed her nose.

Gia turned red. It was obvious to Gia that Persia was not as cool as she thought she was. "I'm sorry, Persia, just forget about what I said. I was only fucking with you."

Instead of leaving the matter alone, Persia raised her hand. "Karen, my Lord," she yelled, "Gia just committed treason against you and the rest of the family."

"Oh my, God, Persia," Gia begged, "Please don't do this."

"Don't tell me not to do this," Persia said getting louder. "She has a right to know what kind of person we have in our camp."

Karen looked at the tension brewing between the girls and she quickly approached them. "What's going on back here?" Karen asked them.

"Tell her," Persia said. "Tell her what you just said to me."

Although Persia was risking Gia's life, that was not her chief aim. She needed Karen to know that she was loyal, and she would do that by throwing the young girl under the bus. If a person's existence wasn't benefiting Persia, then in her opinion their existence didn't matter.

"What did you say, Gia," Karen questioned.

"I...I..."

"She told me I needed to return to my family, and that I shouldn't trust you," Persia said.

Karen's disposition turned dark. She snapped her finger and Oscar rushed over. "Take her to the Soft Room, and dispose of her."

"You got it," Oscar responded, as he took Gia kicking and screaming back into the building.

"You did good," Karen said placing a hand on Persia's shoulder. "Real good."

Karen walked back up to the front of the crowd. She rattled off the names on her clipboard, which was followed with either an A or a B, like she said earlier. Persia didn't feel and ounce of guilt as she stood alone waiting her fate.

Persia figured that the people, who had the letter A behind their name, meant they had AIDS. But, when she heard her name, followed with the letter A, she felt faint. When all of the names were called, fifteen people stood on the B-side, while the majority stood on the A side.

"Everyone with the letter B behind their names, get into the vans," Karen advised.

It took about fifteen minutes for everyone to pile into the vans. When they were completely full, Karen instructed the vans to pull off. When they were gone she readdressed the group. "The people remaining are HIV negative."

Persia exhaled in relief. Although she hadn't slept with Tamir before he died, she did fuck enough losers to win her three rounds of Gonorrhea, and a bout of Trichomoniasis.

"The rest of you can go back into the community center, we have a lot of things to discuss. We need to rebuild this family and talk about our new direction. I have no doubt that after everything we've gone through, that we can do it."

When everybody left, Persia decided to walk up to Karen. Curiosity was killing her and she wanted to know where the B group was going. "What's going to happen to them?" Persia pointed up the street.

"What's going to happen to who, Persia?" Karen looked at the clipboard in her hand.

"Those in the van?"

Karen laughed at the girl's boldness. "They're going to be burned alive. Just like you would've been, if you betrayed this family. Just because you're promised to my son, it would not have stopped me from getting rid of you too. Promises are meant to be broken aren't they?"

Persia's heart stopped for a second. "I would never betray you, or this family," Persia said. "That's why I wanted to talk to you about my mother."

Karen leaned in closer. "What about your mother?"

Persia sighed. "I don't want to tell you this, because it's not my mother's fault. But, if this is my new family you gotta know everything."

"Persia, I'm too busy for games. Get to the point."

Persia swallowed. "I'm sorry," she cleared her throat and rubbed her belly to remind her she was pregnant, in case Karen wanted to hurt her. "It's just that I'm concerned that Mercedes may be trying to use my mother, to get at the Klan. And unlike Gia, I love it here and don't want to leave. But, I'm afraid if my family does something, I'll be banished for good."

"You were talking about Mercedes," Karen said bringing her back to the point. "Why are you worried about her?"

Persia hadn't heard a thing, but that didn't stop her from formulating a good lie. "Mercedes said that she is thinking about kidnapping me, and attacking the Klan, after I have the baby."

Karen's forehead wrinkled and she was breathing heavily. Oscar warned her that the Emerald City women might attack again, but she didn't think it would happen so soon. After all, Persia was still with her, and she could do anything to her if she desired.

With a furrowed brow Karen asked, "Are you sure, Persia?"

"I promise on everything I love, I overheard Mercedes saying that."

"What did your mother say?"

"She didn't seem happy about what Mercedes wanted to do, but I don't think she'll stop her either."

"Don't say anything else to your mother about this, Persia. I'm going to see how things play out."

PITBULLS IN A SKIRT 4

She placed a firm hand on Persia's clavicle. "You did good by coming to me. I'm very proud of you. Don't worry about anything else though. I'll take it from here."

CHAPTER 17
MERCEDES

I'm home playing Rihanna's new CD, and me and Toi are drinking Merlot in the living room, while we watch Lloyd fry chicken in the kitchen.

"He's fine as shit ain't he," I say to her, after crossing my legs. "I can look at him all day."

"He's fine alright," Toi says. "But I smell a dangerous territory that you're moving into. Just because an idea is bright, don't mean it'll help you see straight."

"What you talking about now, girl," I laugh.

"Mercedes, you have bought yourself a slave," she leans back into the sofa. "I hope you know that."

"And?"

"And you can't do people like that, and not for the reasons you think neither. You gonna end up falling for him, or somebody else, and when you can't get them to act the way you want them too, you're gonna snap."

"Toi, please."

"I'm serious, Mercedes. You're conditioning yourself to avoid rejection, but life is about rejection and choices. That's how you build your muscles for it."

"I'm just having fun," I say. "Ain't no harm in that."

"Mercedes, I love a boy toy just as much as the next bitch, but you're putting him up in your house and shit. If you want to fuck the dude on the outside, and not call him afterwards, that's big girl shit. But you have moved him into your world, Mercedes, into your home. As fine as he is, I'm begging you to please get rid of him."

I laugh hysterically. "I'm not going to fall for him if that's what you're worried about. Trust me, I'm done with love."

"Mercedes, you never took the time to get over Cameron."

I frown and look at this bitch like she crazy…'cause she is. "Toi, if I recall you were fucking with Cameron last, and the next thing I know you were with Michael. So what you talking about?"

Toi whispers, "I'm talking about you. And the fact that the moment the relationship was over with Cameron, you married Derrick. And when Derrick started cheating, you started over-loving and smothering C. And now that Derrick is dead, you got some half naked man in your kitchen cooking chicken who you paying. If you don't take time to find out who you are, you'll never know what you really want. That goes for you, Yvette and your home-girl Carissa too."

"Who are you Dr. Phil?"

She giggles. "For you to be my friend, I would've hoped you'd be a little more original."

"You know what I mean."

"I do," she laughs. "But I'm not Dr. Phil and I'm not trying to be. I'm just a girl who ended up in a bad place some years back, trying to find love from outside sources. It took a year by myself, for me to find out what I needed to be happy. That's when I met Michael."

"And you chose a nigga who loves porn to be by your side?"

"No, I love porn," she corrects me. "And he accepts me. He fucks me hard like I like. He nourishes my dreams like I like, and he tells me every time he looks in my eyes how much he loves me. But he does it without words, 'Cedes. I can feel it when I'm around him. He accepts all of my garbage, and he still loves me the way I am. But he a real nigga too so he gonna speak his mind and sometimes he has to tell me no, and I respect him enough to accept it. And, I just want the same thing for you."

I hear Toi talking, and maybe part of what she is saying is true. But, I can't be alone right now. If I'm by myself, I might snap, and right now I have to be strong. There are so many things I have to do. I have a business to run, a relationship with my children to mend, and friends to support. Now is not the right time to be in my head dealing with the serious shit.

"How does this look?" Monie says exiting the back of my condo. She spins around in the black

True Religion jeans I bought her, along with the red Gucci blouse. "Dumb?"

"You look beautiful," Lloyd says from the kitchen. He wipes his hands on the pink apron he's wearing.

Monie blushes at him.

"What do you think Ms. Mercedes and Ms. Toi?"

"I think C 'bout to lose his fucking mind," I say. "And you damn sure won't be leaving out no house, no time soon. Remember what I said though," I point at her, "for the next week or so you are not available. You cook his meals, tend to his basic needs, but then you out the house."

"Where am I going to go?" she asks.

"You come over here," I say. "At least you don't have to worry about C popping up. The last person he wants to see is me."

Toi touches my leg softly. I sigh thinking of our broken relationship.

"But I help him run Camelot on the weekends."

"First off when you working in Camelot, you are going to wear one of the twenty outfits I bought you. You gotta always dress like this."

Monie leans in closer. "Ms. Mercedes, I can't dress like this at work. I gotta check them niggas on the block about C's money sometimes. I can't do that in no high heels and shit."

"Do you know that when me and my girls were holding down Emerald, we did it in high heels, and designer purses? Just because we ran a drug operation didn't mean our looks suffered. C needs to be thinking about you, even while you working and your gear is essential to the mind play."

"She's right," Lloyd says wiping his forehead with his arm. "A man respects a woman who dresses sexy all the time. You need to stay on your A-game if you want to land a baller. Mercedes knows what she's talking about."

"That's right, baby, but how 'bout you flip my chicken over," I tell him. "It's burning."

"I'm on it," he says under his breath.

Monie takes off in the back room to prevent from laughing out loud I guess.

"You wrong as shit for that one," Toi laughs under her breath. "Why you do that man like that?"

"I pay the nigga to cook, not think."

When there is a knock at the door I get up.

"I think that's my brother," Lloyd says to me from the kitchen. "He's coming to pick me up. We taking my mother out for her birthday. Remember I was telling you about that, Mercedes?"

I roll my eyes. "Oh yeah, my chicken done?"

"I'm pulling it out now," he says.

I walk towards the door. "What you doing later, Toi? Because I gotta get up with Carissa. She wants to talk about Persia again."

"If you putting me out I guess I'm going to see Mike," she laughs.

"Girl you can stay over here if you want to," I continue opening the door. "Just let me—"

I don't believe in love at first sight. Even when I met Cameron, at first I wasn't interested in giving him the time of day. He had to work my heart over hard to get me to see that he was the one for me. I felt he was too attractive, and had too many women on his dick. I wasn't trying to be a part of his fan club.

But now, I think there is something to this love at first sight thing. Because when I look into the eyes of the stranger at my door, I feel transformed. Like we loved before, maybe in a different lifetime.

Jackson is about 6'4, with a baldhead. He has a silky black goatee, and his complexion is the color of wet brown sugar.

"H-hello," I stutter. "You are?"

He doesn't answer me right away. Instead he's staring into my eyes. I think he feels the same way.

"Jackson," Lloyd says walking up behind me. His hand touches the lower part of my back and I'm immediately annoyed. "This is my lady Mercedes that I was telling you about."

I extend my hand, and Jackson looks into my eyes. "This is your lady?" He takes my hand and goose bumps travel up my arm.

"Actually they are friends," Toi says walking behind us. "With a good understanding." She hugs me. "Anyway I'm out, Mercedes. I know you gonna call me later."

She looked out majorly with that move, because Lloyd was trying to cock block by saying we were together and shit. Anyway it's a lie. He isn't my man, he's my slave. There's a difference.

"Okay, Toi," I say to her. "I'll get up with you later."

When she walks out, the three of us are standing alone in the doorway. Jackson and I are looking at one another, while Lloyd is somewhere behind me.

"Well, I'll be back later," Lloyd says, breaking us out of our gaze. "I'll call you if I'm running too late." He tries to kiss me but I back up.

I want him to kill himself. Just keel over right here. Jackson could possibly be the love of my life, and I'm wasting time on him. I gotta find a way to get rid of Lloyd and get to know Jackson a little better. I guess I have my hands full. Don't I?

CHAPTER 18

CARISSA

"Yvette, I'm sorry about your dogs," I say to her on the phone as I steer my car on the way to the BWK compound. "I know how much you loved them."

She's crying hard. This is the first time I've heard her cry since we buried Kenyetta.

I was on my way to visit my daughter, when Yvette called and told me what Chris did. Yvette is my friend, but I feel like she's leaving something out. I know Chris, and for the most part she seemed low-key and non-confrontational. Something had to happen for Chris to make such a move, especially when she knew how violent my friends could be. Anyway the last thing I heard regarding their relationship, was that Chris had moved on and was about to marry some chick.

"You should've seen the look in her eyes, Carissa," Yvette says sniffling. "I'm telling you I've never seen her look at me like that before. She hates me, like I was a born enemy. We done with each other for sure now."

I make a left. "Yvette, what made her go off like that? It ain't like Chris to move in that manner. She acted like she loved you too much."

"You know why she did that shit, I threw her old book out."

My jaw drops. Throwing the old book out means she got rid of someone she loved. And since I figured she was talking about Chris' new girlfriend, I wondered why Yvette would do that. It wasn't like Yvette didn't move on with Judah. As a matter of fact she told me that Judah was on his way over her house at the moment. So what she wants with Chris?

"What do you mean you threw her old book out?"

"It was dumb, I know it," Yvette says. "But I feel like I'm going through some sort of midlife crisis. I thought that type of shit happened in your forties. I didn't want her to have a girlfriend, or anybody else for that matter."

I'm mad at her. I'm mad at Mercedes too. Since when has murder been the main thing to do when you have problems? Mercedes killed Derrick, and now Yvette killed Lace. Human life is worthless to them. My friends are turning into some sick kind of Killer Klan. I feel like I don't know them anymore.

"I just think we need a vacation, Yvette. All of us. It would be nice if we could bring the kids too."

"Whenever you're ready, I'm with it."

"Maybe we can do it after the wedding," I tell her.

"If there's going to be a wedding," she says. "I don't want to talk about that right now though. How is everything going with Persia? Is stuff moving smoother with my fake ass sister Karen running things?"

"I don't know what's going on, 'Vette, to tell you the truth. I called the Compound earlier to confirm the meet up I had with Persia tonight, but nobody answered the phone. Then I blew up Persia's cell phone, and she didn't answer either. I'm nervous."

"They ain't fucking with that girl, especially considering we haven't given them all of the money yet. They on their asses over there, they need that cash."

"The best thing you could've told me was to stretch their paper out. I hate to think what would have happened if I would've given her the entire three hundred stacks like she wanted."

Yvette laughs. "You don't have to think about what would've happened because I nipped that shit in the bud. When Mercedes told me you were withdrawing the cash I stopped her." Mercedes handles our big money in overseas accounts. We keep but so much on us at a time. "Anyway, Judah just got here. Call me back later to let me know how things go tonight."

"Aight," I say hanging up.

After parking my car in front of the compound, I walk to the main building's door. The same man who usually lets me in steps outside and blocks my entrance. I glance at the gold Bulova watch on my arm. "It's five o'clock pm, and I have a meeting with my daughter this evening," I tell him. "Is she here?"

"Things have changed," he says dryly.

I frown at him. "What do you mean that things have changed?"

He digs into his jean pocket and hands me a sheet of crumpled paper. "Your daughter is at this location. You need to go there."

I read the white piece of paper, and fear washes over me. "What do you mean go there? Where is Karen? We had an arrangement and nobody told me things would be changing."

"Somebody just did," he says.

"Is something wrong with my daughter? I mean is she okay?"

"The location, ma'am."

"If somebody has hurt her, I'll be back here."

He laughs at me, walks back inside and closes the door. I rush to my car and enter the address into my GPS. I don't know why but I think I should've called my girls. What if I'm walking into an ambush?

At moments like this, I blame Lavelle for being a bad man, boyfriend and father. Had he not took Thick's side, and chose money over our family, I wouldn't be going through this shit alone. Persia is way out of hand right now, and if he was in the picture, I have a feeling it wouldn't be that way. She needs a father's love. She needs her family.

When I finally make it to the address on the piece of paper, I notice it's a set of office buildings. I get out, walk to the building, and then the suite. I knock on the closed door and Karen says, "It's open."

When I plod inside I see Persia and Karen sitting on the other end of a long brown table. I sit down in the seat next to the door, and look at Persia. She's wearing a pink long dress, with a massive white bow in front of it. I wonder why they dress her so juvenile, and more importantly why she allows them too.

"Why are we here?" I look at Persia and then Karen. "I thought we agreed to meet in the compound." They are sitting across the table like mother and daughter, and I feel like the deadbeat father who is allowed supervised visitation.

"Things have changed," Karen says with the red book in front of her.

"The nigga at the door told me that shit already," I say. "I mean did I do something wrong?"

Silence.

"Persia, is something wrong?" I ask her. "Is the baby okay?" I eye her huge stomach.

"I'm fine," Persia says rolling her eyes. "How is Mercedes? The only person in the world you care about."

I frown. "Persia, what is going on? I told you before that I won't allow Mercedes to come in the middle of our relationship. I also spoke to her the other day and explained that it was wrong for her to taunt you. If she does it again, I'm done with her all together, but we shouldn't allow her to come in between our relationship."

"Taunt me?" Persia giggles. "What that word mean?"

"Carissa, how do you like the arrangement I set up for you?" Karen interrupts.

I sigh. "What do you mean by that?"

"Haven't I done all that I could, to make sure that you and your daughter maintain a relationship?"

"Haven't you also taken my money?"

Karen sits back in the chair and frowns at me. "It's important that you understand that my kindness shouldn't be taken for a weakness."

"I just want the relationship with my daughter you promised. I don't want any trouble."

"What about your friends? Do they feel the same way?"

"Of course. They know how important it is for me to have a bond with Persia. I've expressed it to them in great detail. Trust me, you don't have to worry about my friends." I receive a text message in the middle of my plea. "Give me a second," I raise my index finger, "I have to check on this."

I pull my cell out of my purse. There's a message from C. It reads:

My man told me a few suits have been around Tyland and Emerald. We might have to put things on hold.

My head feels like it tightens. One of my biggest fears, and also one of the reasons I wanted to get out of the drug game, was that sooner than later we would all be given indictments. And now it's a possibility that it may happen. This fake meeting can wait. I have to get up with my girls like yesterday.

CHAPTER 19

PERSIA

After the meeting, Persia decided to sneak into Karen's office. Ever since she first laid eyes on the red book, she had been obsessed with finding out what was inside of it. Anything she could pull to use Karen as her weapon she was willing to do. Since she knew the key was in the desk, she retrieved it and hustled toward the chest against the wall.

When the chest was open, she pulled the book out, and looked at the door. With little time to spare, she sat on the floor to go through the pages. She knew this move could not only get her in trouble with the Klan if she was caught, but also killed. That didn't stop her. She was use to living dangerously.

The moment she flipped the book open, the office door opened. Nervous, she farted on the floorboards as she waited for her fate. When Oscar walked inside, she immediately started crying. She figured with him she could take the sympathy route, being as though he liked her so much.

"Please don't tell on me, Oscar." She stood up and rubbed her pregnant belly. "I just wanted to see what was in the book. I know it was wrong."

Oscar walked up to her, and rubbed her face with the back of his hand. "Calm down, Persia." He pressed his glasses against his nose. "You're going to mess around and have that baby before it's time."

"I can't calm down. I know this is wrong," she looked down at the book, "but I let my curiosity get the better of me. I know you're angry at me but please don't tell your mother or the other members of the Klan. I'm begging you."

Oscar looked down at her. She looked so vulnerable, and so sneaky that he was immediately turned on. From the first day that he saw her face, when Tamir brought her into the Klan, he wanted to have her. Besides, Tamir was the leader and he always got first dibs on the women, Oscar wanted it to be his turn. Now that Karen was at the seat of power, he could get who and what he wanted. He certainly wouldn't risk getting her in trouble, by telling his mother about her sneaky behavior.

"What were you doing with the book?" He looked down at it on the floor.

"I wanted to know your beliefs. I wanted to make sure that I'm doing the right things so I don't get thrown out like the others, like Gia."

"Well you shouldn't be in here," he picked the book up. "If they knew you were in here, you could get hurt." He walked the book over to the chest.

"Oscar, let me see the book," she said touching his hand. "Please." She laid her head on his chest. "I just want to see a few pages, that's all."

"I can't, Persia," he whispered. "If somebody comes in here and sees this, things could get serious, and I could get into trouble right along with you."

"I thought you were in charge," she pouted.

"I am," he said upon receiving the blow to his ego.

"Then let me see it. Please, Oscar, I'll do almost anything you say," Persia said.

"Anything?"

"Yes, including sneaking into the bathroom when you ask me, at meal time."

"Don't lie to me," he said.

"I'm serious, Oscar. I wouldn't lie to you. You got this over me now. You could blackmail me if you want too."

"Okay, but don't be in here too long. You got five minutes and after that I'm coming back in here for you, Persia." He grabbed her shoulders, pulled her toward him and pressed his dry lips against her face. Afterwards he left the office.

"Yuck," Persia said shaking her head. She wiped her lips with her knuckles.

When he was gone she scanned through the book as quickly as she could. She realized she wouldn't remember some of the interesting points, so she had to think. So when she spotted the Xerox machine against the wall, she decided to make a few copies of the important passages to take with her. When she was done, she returned the book to the chest, locked the door and returned the key to the desk.

When she left out, she didn't see Roman and Lance in the hallway.

But they saw her.

CHAPTER 20
YVETTE

I'm standing in the doorway of Mama's Kitchen, and a tingling sensation courses up from my ankles, to my knees, and makes it difficult for me to stand up straight.

I'm holding onto my cell phone, until it somersaults from my hand, and crashes to the ground. That's the second iPhone I've bought in six months, and yet the screen fractures upon impact. I look into the restaurant, for my friends, and my face feels frozen in fear. Mercedes and Carissa observe me from inside, and rush toward me, just before I fall to the warm ground.

"Yvette, what the fuck is going on," Mercedes asks, as she pulls me to my feet by stuffing her hands under my underarm.

"You're scaring me," Carissa says, as she lifts me up by the other underarm.

My gun falls from the back of my jeans, and makes a thud to the ground. Mercedes quickly picks it up, looks around to see who's watching us, and stuffs it inside her purse.

"You tripping hard now," Mercedes says to me. "Let's go to your truck before somebody calls them Justice boys on us."

◄┈┈┈┈┈┈┈┈┈┈┈┈┈┈┈┈┈┈┈┈►

A twisted line of sweat dampens Mercedes' forehead. "I don't understand what you're saying," she covers her quivering pink lips. She's in the passenger seat of my truck, looking at me with disbelief. "But, how did this happen? I…I don't understand."

"I don't know either I say," in a low voice. "I was walking into the restaurant to meet ya'll, when I got a text from one of Judah's boys saying that he had been indicted." I look back at Carissa. "For all I know we up next."

"Oh my God," Carissa says as tears roll down her face and dangle from her chin. "I can't…we can't…go to jail. We just can't." She wipes the tears from her face. "What's going to happen to our family? What's going to happen to us? Huh, Yvette? What they gonna do if they lock us up?"

"Gee, Carissa, I'm sure they'll slap us on the hands, give us probation and send us along our merry way," I say sarcastically. "Bitch, I don't know what the fuck will happen," I scream hitting the steering wheel. "This is my first time being involved in any of this type shit too!"

Carissa breaks into an ugly cry.

"What exactly did his boy say," Mercedes asks me softly. When Carissa starts hyperventilating in the back she says, "Car, you gotta calm down. We gonna be okay, we just gotta get ourselves together." Carissa calms down a little. "Now, 'Vette, what exactly did his boy say?"

I pull my phone from my purse and read the text verbatim, through the shattered iPhone screen. *'Dis Boots...Judah's man. Dey came to his house and gave him papers.'* I look at Mercedes. "That was it."

Mercedes sighs and says, "This is the worst thing that could've happened to us. I mean, I can't believe this shit is real. All the years we were doing business, it was in the back of my mind but I never actually thought it would happen. That we could get indicted. I mean, we been paying the police since they first opened Emerald City's gates. Who the fuck talking?"

"You mean Dreyfus was paying the police," I say to her. "After we killed him, a lot of cops lost their houses, and side bitches too, because we weren't greasing their palms the same way anymore."

Carissa's face hardens. "Why? Why we stop paying them?"

"I don't know," I shrug. "We just did. Them niggas was getting too greedy anyway. Plus Kenyetta was on that before she died and we didn't assign the job again."

Carissa's face brightens with understanding. "This is it," she smiles. "We actually lost Emerald City." I feel like cracking the happy grin on her face.

"I can't lose Emerald," I say honestly. "Do you hear me? I can't lose Emerald. I don't know who I am without the city. All of my blood, sweat and tears have been poured into that operation. I don't have nothing left without it. I fell in love with Thick in Emerald, I killed Thick in Emerald and I became the beast I am today in Emerald." I throw my hands up in the air. "Fuck, I even met ya'll in Emerald. Emerald represents who I am, I can't lose it."

Mercedes places her hand softly on my knee. "We may have lost it already, baby. Maybe you should come to terms with the fact that it's time to let it go."

The fear of losing Emerald squeezes my chest. "It's easy for you to say, you got kids," I yell at her. "Both of ya'll." I look back at Carissa. "But who I have? What I got to show for all of the years I've thrown into that business? Huh? What I got?"

"You got us, Yvette," Carissa says to me. "We love you harder than we could love a family member with our own blood. You not going through this shit alone. We going through it too. So we need to toughen up, and push through."

"She's' right," Mercedes says. "Shit is going to be rough without Emerald. It's like closing a be-loved business, but its time to let Emerald go. We have to turn our attention to what counts. Right now we have to find C, Chante, Persia and Treasure. We got to bring everybody together in case these indictments do come down. We have to quarterback our next moves."

I exhale deeply. "How much money we got overseas?" I say to Mercedes.

"Let me check on that right now," she responds pulling her iPad out of her purse.

As she checks on the status of our accounts my heart breaks. I can't help but think about what Chris said before she left my house the other day. She said I was going to pay for taking a mother from her child. I knew my karma would come sooner or later, but I never thought it would come in the form of indictments.

I don't have no skillsets. I don't have an education or a high school diploma. I'm just a gangster, who knows how to pull guns and command soldiers. Even though I know I got at least fifteen million dollars in the overseas accounts what was I going to do with it? It was never about the money for me. It was about building, creating and running a drug operation. I love that shit more than I love to bust a nut.

I'm not no sadity-type bitch who can sit up on some yellow beach, look at green water, and sip Pina Coladas all day. I like the grit and the grind of the streets. I like murder and mayhem. I like setting up plays to deal with thieves and niggas trying to take shit from us. I love the fucking hustle! My girls could keep the limelight.

"What's going on?" Mercedes asks someone on the phone. The concern in her voice wakes me from my thoughts. “Check that shit again,” she yells to the caller. “Fuck you talking about?”

Silence.

I look back at Carissa. The terror in her eyes makes my stomach churn so I turn around and look at the streets instead.

“I’ll call back. Thank you,” Mercedes says ending the call.

I sit up in the driver’s seat and look over at her. “Everything okay with the accounts?”

“It’s g…e.” Her voice is so hoarse that I can’t make out the words.

“What?”

“I said,” she swallows. “It’s gone.”

“W-what is gone?” Carissa says touching her shoulder. “T-the money is gone where? To another account?”

Mercedes looks at her, and then at me. “Everything is gone. All of our money.”

I feel like God has picked up my truck, sat it on the tip of his index finger, and spun it around rapidly. Everything is rotating so fast now, that I feel dizzy. I open my truck, and throw up everything I ate earlier. I’m doing it so long, that I begin heaving dry air. When I don’t have anything else to regurgitate, I keep the door open for a while and take in the cool breeze. The air mixed with the fumes from my engine, nauseate me again. When I feel Mercedes’ warm hand on my lower back, I inhale and close the door.

I look ahead of me, wipe my mouth with my knuckles, and lower my head. Staring into my lap I say, "What is happening to us?"

"I don't know," Mercedes says. "But I don't think we should go back home. If we are going to be arrested, and the Feds have seized our accounts, we need to set up our families before they take us down. We gotta get lawyers and prepare our defense."

"We have nothing," I say to myself. "We have nothing. We were millionaires one second, and now we're broker than we have ever been."

Carissa sighs and leans back into the seat. "How much cash ya'll have that you can lay your hands on?"

"I got fifty thousand in the back of my truck, in my gym bag," I say.

"And I got the fifty thousand I was going to give Karen for Persia," Carissa replies.

"I'm not sure but I think I got about five thousand under my car seat," Mercedes says. "I usually have more, but I never got a chance to replenish my shopping money so it's all I have left."

For some reason I burst into laughter. I laugh so hard my stomach muscles feel tender. "I can't believe it, what we use to think of as little money, is now all the money we got left in the world between us. Karma just gave us her ass to kiss."

Carissa shakes her head and says, "Outside of the money we can lay our hands on, we actually broke. But, we still richer than some folks I suppose."

"Not by our standards," I say dryly.

"It's nothing we can do about it now," Mercedes says. "They took our money and now we gotta pull our lives together, while we still free and out in these streets. First we need to bring our family together and we have to go into hiding." Mercedes picks up her cell phone. She waits for a minute and says, "Toi, I need your help." She looks at me. "Me and my girls need to go into hiding. Can you help us out?" Mercedes gets silent. "I really appreciate it." She hangs up. "Toi says she'll meet us at her apartment. She got a small one bedroom crib, but I'm sure she will put us up some kind of way."

"She know I'm coming?" I ask.

"Yes."

"And she's okay with that?"

"Yvette, Toi is cool people. She don't harbor ill will and she definitely doesn't hold grudges. I need her help and she has agreed to come through for us. *All of us.* You my family so that means you too."

I know Toi is cool. I really do. But, I don't know why I feel like something else is up with her. Mercedes says I have a problem with people who have a strong will like I do. I beg to differ. My antennas are up with Toi, and I don't know why. I'm sure I'm on to something and in time, it will be revealed.

"If you like her I love her," I lie. "Besides, what other choice do we have now?"

CHAPTER 21
MERCEDES

I'm sitting in the passenger seat of Yvette's truck with my jaw damn near in my lap. We're following Toi in her older model white BMW, to her house, a place she says we're welcome to hide until we figure things out. The thing is I knew about her apartment out Maryland, but we've pulled up into some exclusive suburb in Baltimore called Kingston, about an hour away from her apartment. The houses over here look like mini-mansions, and I'm confused. How can she afford to live over here?

"I thought you said your girl worked at the Social Security Administration out Baltimore," Yvette says to me steering her truck. "What gives?"

"She does," I reply. "I been to her office and everything to have lunch. Met her co-workers and some more shit. I don't know what this is about, but whatever it is, she doing a good damn job of it."

Before long we pull up on this gorgeous white stone mansion with three garages. One of the garage doors open and Toi pulls her car inside.

"This shit is beyond weird," Carissa says in the back seat. "Your girl may have a 9 to 5, but she got another hustle too."

"Mommy, who lives here?" Treasure says sitting on Carissa's lap in the backseat.

"I don't know, baby," Carissa says looking at the house. "I don't know."

We went to pick up Treasure, Carissa's youngest daughter earlier today from her friend Bria's house. I had already sent the bus ticket for Chante to come home from school, and would be picking her up later at the bus station. Now I have to get my hands on C, who I'm sure won't come easily. And we'll also have to kidnap Persia from the Klan. Our life has been reduced to a pile of wet shit, and I have a feeling it's only gonna get worse.

"Come on inside," Toi says from the passenger side window. "Everything is set up for you all."

We pile out of the truck and follow her into the house. I'm immediately blown away at the expensive décor, the vaulted ceilings and the beautiful crystal and gold chandeliers. The cherry wood spiral staircase is breathtaking, and I feel like I'm in the home of some Hollywood starlet. For all I know, maybe I am.

"Come this way," Toi says breaking me out of my gaze. "We're going downstairs."

"Mercedes, what's up with your girl?" Yvette whispers to me. She looks up at the paintings on the ceiling from the great Michelangelo. "Because it don't look like she being truthful with you."

I love Yvette harder than I could love another female, but sometimes she is too skeptical of people. I don't care what Toi got going on, on the side, at this point she is willing to help us, and we need to accept her assistance. Deep inside I think Yvette is worried that Toi will try to get into my head, and take me away from her. But if my own nigga Cameron couldn't do it, and I loved him to death, what makes her think another female could?

We walk down some cream plush carpeted steps to a large basement. The scent of a berry air freshener enters my nose and makes me feel at home. Inside of the basement is a theater size TV on the wall, and a fully stocked bar. But here's the kicker, in the middle of the floor are six twin-sized beds, with frames and headboards to match.

"Toi, you're my girl," I say to her from my heart, "and you gotta know I appreciate all of this shit, but when are you going to be real with me, and tell me what you really in to?"

She smiles. "All generals don't wear their stripes on their arms, for all to see."

"I get that," I respond. "But this shit is a bit confusing." I throw my purse on one of the beds and spin around in place. "The only thing I knew about you was that you had a small apartment out Maryland." I look into her eyes. "Now you taking me to a plush ass mansion, complete with beds for me and my friends to sleep in. What's up?"

Toi sits on one of the beds and looks up at me. "Mercedes, I'm one of you."

"What does that mean?"

"Do I gotta state the obvious?" She sighs. "I'm one of you and I always have been. But I don't showcase what I make, or how much money I earn to the world. Yeah I love fly shoes, and designer bags, but I'm content with pushing an old ass BMW, if it means I can live in a home like this without having to worry about a nigga waiting in my bushes trying to rob or kill me. I live low-key, but that's how I prefer it. It's not because I have to. I stay at the apartment in Maryland when I gotta go to work during the week, and come here on the weekends."

"But why didn't you tell me? It makes me think you don't trust me."

"You wouldn't be here if I didn't trust you," she says. "And I didn't tell you because you didn't ask."

"This is some bullshit," Yvette says. "I knew this bitch wasn't real. Now will you trust me when I say I know what I'm talking about, Mercedes?"

Toi stands up and approaches Yvette and my forehead tightens. I immediately stand in front of Yvette to protect her. I'm always protecting her. "Move, Mercedes, me and your girl have to have a conversation, and we gotta do it now, before we go any further."

"Toi, I don't think—,"

"When you needed me I came," Toi says to me. "I didn't give you a hard time and I didn't tell you to leave your girl at home. Despite it being obvious that she has a fucking problem with me. Now I'm asking for a few seconds with Yvette. Can you respect it or not? If not, you gotta leave my house, and you gotta do it now. Accept this time there is no turning back, our friendship is severed when you leave out of those doors. No comebacks."

I look her into her eyes and move out of her way.

"Yvette, you not gonna come into my house and disrespect me," Toi says. "So lets get that straight right now."

"You get respect when you give it, Boss Lady," Yvette jokes.

"So what's on your mind," Toi says. "Don't beat around the bush just say the shit, Yvette."

"I know a hustler when I see one," Yvette says.

"Oh do you?" Toi laughs. "Because at Mercedes' crib you were all too content with calling me a square."

"And now I see you not," Yvette laughs."

"Don't get mad at me because your piggy bank is bare," Toi says. "That was on you not me. Maybe if you weren't busy showboating you wouldn't be facing possible indictments."

That hurt.

"You don't know what you talking about," Yvette replies. "You could never reach the levels I have. We were making millions…millions!"

"That's your problem, you looking with your jealous heart and not your eyes and mind. Who the fuck do you think supplied Cameron when him and I were together? Dreyfus cut the nigga off, and it was me who kept the money flowing in his pockets. My product…my package."

"But how?" I ask her.

"Through my friends," Toi tells me. She looks at her watch. "Actually they should be here in a minute." She looks at Yvette. "So what do you say, you wanna put your feelings aside, and get along? Or do you want to exit up the stairs to the left? The choice is yours."

My heart is beating wildly in my chest. Yvette doesn't have anywhere to go, that is safe anyway. Plus Judah is in jail. Toi is looking out majorly because we were the only family Yvette has. But, her pride is as big as the Goodyear Blimp, and she would rather lick spit off the D.C. streets, than to take a handout from anyone else.

"I'll chill," Yvette says.

Toi smiles and says. "Great, let me go upstairs to see where my friends are. I'll be back in a minute."

When she is gone I say, "Thanks, Yvette. I know that was hard."

"It's hard but I'm not stupid," she says sitting on one of the beds. "We don't have a choice. Until I can come up with another plan, we need to fall back and chill. And I want us to do that together, although I still don't like your home girl."

"I do," Treasure says when she finds a Wii video game console. "I like her TV too." She turns the TV on with the remote, and begins to play some videogame.

"I like her too," Carissa says. "She knows how to help a bitch out in a bind, she's time enough for 'Vette and she seems real. That's all she needs to win my vote." Carissa sighs. "Now we gotta get our hands on Persia and C."

"Well Persia won't have a choice," Yvette says. "We been polite to her up to this point, now it's time to take her by force."

"I agree," I say. "And hopefully C will come without problems too."

"C not stupid," Yvette says, "he not trying to go to jail if He can help it. He'll come."

A minute later Toi comes back down stairs followed with four women. They look like bosses and all four of them are stunningly beautiful. The first girl has brown wavy hair, and she's wearing a black tight t-shirt, army fatigues pants and some black high top Louis Vuitton sneakers. They came out in 2009, but they still looked new. Followed behind her was this beautiful white girl with red hair. She was kind of tall, and the blue jeans she's wearing made her ass look extra big. Behind her was another black girl with short red curly hair and a lot of tattoos on her arms and neck. Behind her was another girl with light brown shoulder length hair, and a wide smile.

"Mercedes, I want you to meet my friends," Toi says. "This is Bambi Kennedy," she says pointing to the girl in the fatigues. "This is Scarlett Kennedy," she says pointing to the white girl. "This is Denim Kennedy," she says pointing to the girl with the red hair and tattoos over her body. "And this is Race Kennedy," she continues pointing to the last girl with the shoulder length brown hair. "They are known as the Pretty Kings."

"The Pretty Kings?" I frown. "I heard about them."

"Don't believe most of what you hear, unless you hear it from me first," Bambi says smiling. I like her immediately. I know from jump that she's the boss.

"Bambi, these are my good friends Mercedes, Yvette and Carissa," Toi says.

"I'm not her good friend," Yvette interrupts. "I'm their good friend." Yvette points to us.

What the fuck is wrong with Yvette? She's tripping hard now. Why can't she see people are trying to help us? She's about to ruin this for everybody.

Bambi laughs, "Well I hope you are good friends of Toi's, otherwise you are wasting my time and hers. Now my friend told us you were in trouble, and since we have a mutual acquaintance, who is currently in a bind, we decided to see how we could help you."

"A mutual acquaintance?" Yvette replies.

"Yes, Judah was one of my customers," Bambi says.

"You know Judah, Toi?" I ask.

"Yes."

"I didn't know."

"You didn't ask," Toi winks.

"We understand that he was just indicted," Bambi says. "Now we aren't worried about him talking, he's cut from a different cloth. But we wanted to meet the people who he does business with, to be sure you are just as stand up as your captain."

"Are you asking us if we snitches?" Yvette says stepping up to her with an attitude.

The moment Yvette moves, the girl with the brown bob pulls a shiny .45 on Yvette with a crystal handle. The smile on Race's face is wiped off, and Carissa and me pull our weapons too.

Treasure starts crying hysterically.

"Little girl, everything is okay," Bambi says to her. Treasure doesn't stop crying. "Trust me, everything is okay, and nobody is going to get hurt." Treasure stops crying. Bambi faces her goon. "Lower your weapon, Race."

"Not until I blow this bitch's face off," Race responds looking at Yvette.

"You threatening me?" Yvette says cocking her weapon.

"Lower your gun, Race," Bambi replies with more authority.

Race lowers her weapon.

Bambi looks at Yvette and says, "I called of my dog, now call off yours."

Yvette bites her bottom lip and says, "Put 'em down girls." We do.

"Now, let me clear something up," Bambi says. "I'm not one of them corner kids you probably entertain yourself with on a daily basis. I'm a gangster, ex-military, and the realest bitch you've ever seen in your life. Present company included."

"I doubt that very seriously," Yvette says.

"Well you shouldn't," Bambi smirks. "If you knew me you wouldn't be so foolish with your mouth play, baby gangster. Now you and your girls real fly with the guns, and I respect that, but we not the enemy. And if me questioning your loyalty offends you, get over it, because it's only because I don't know you." Bambi looks at Toi. "Now my girl only deals with standup bitches, and if she thought you were anything less, we wouldn't be in your company right now. But I must tell you, the next time a gun is drawn in my presence, somebody dies."

"You right about that shit," Yvette says.

"Good," Bambi nods. "So there's no more confusion. Now, there was a question on the table before we began the dick-measuring contest. Indictments have gone out and I want to know if we can count on you and your crew to hold your tongues."

"We don't move like that," I say grinding my teeth. "Me and my girls are married to this game. We wouldn't embarrass it by singing to the DEA."

"Good," Bambi nods. "I think you all should stay here for as long as you can. I'll find out what I can about what the DEA knows. In the meantime, we'll be in contact. Stay free, ladies."

"Let me walk them upstairs," Toi says to me. "I'll be back."

Race looks at Yvette one last time, before they disappear. When they are all gone Carissa walks over to Treasure to calm her down. I walk up to Yvette.

"Why do you gotta act all wild and shit all the time?" I ask her. "These people are helping us, and you could've gotten us killed."

"Keep your eyes open, Mercedes," Yvette says to me. "Something else is going on around here. And pretty soon we gonna find out what it is too."

CHAPTER 22

LIL C

Lil C walked into his apartment in Camelot with a heavy heart and mind. Business in Camelot had ceased to exist, and he was already feeling the anxiousness about not being able to make money. They couldn't do shit with the swarm of white people in suits, that had taken over the property. All he wanted to do was get up under Monie, go to sleep, and wake up with a plan for tomorrow.

He yawned, and walked back to his bedroom, only to see Monie walking out with her purse in hand. He had noticed that over the past few weeks, Monie had lost a little weight, but now that she was wearing the tight designer blue jeans, he saw her slimmer physique. Now he wanted some pussy.

"Where you going?" he asked rubbing his hand over her thick thigh.

"Out," Monie said going through her purse. "I put your fried chicken in paper bags on the stove, that way they'll stay nice and crispy. Some steamed broccoli with cheddar cheese is in the pot on the stove, and the rice is in the steamer." She kissed him

on the cheek. "I'll be back." She walked around him and toward the door.

C turned around and followed her. "Monie, I was kind of hoping you could chill with me tonight."

"Sorry, C, I got plans," Monie said unlocking the door.

"Well break 'em," he replied. "For me."

"I can't do that," Monie turned the doorknob.

"Monie, I'm having a bad day today," C admitted. "I'm not pumping in Camelot no more, I got word from Yvette that my mother wants us to go into hiding, because our connect was indicted, my head his hurting and I got a lot of shit on my mind. All I want to do is be with you, and get in the bed. Please, baby. Stay with me."

Monie was stunned. In all of the years she'd known C, she'd never seen him so vulnerable. Sure she could've played it like the script Mercedes had given her, and left him by his lonesome, but she loved C, and she wanted to be there for him.

Before giving in, Monie thought about Mercedes' current love situation. She wanted to be sure she was the best person to give advice. So Monie played the tapes back in her mind.

She killed Cameron. She had killed Derrick. And, she bought herself a love slave. Perhaps taking advice from Ms. Mercedes, and playing dumb games is immature.

Monie decided to cut the games and keep it real with C. So it was time to talk again from her heart.

"C, I can't be your..."

"I was wrong, Monie," C said walking up to her. "I was wrong for how I treated you since I moved you in. I've been on some different shit since I found out my mother killed my pops, and I been treating you like shit. I'm gonna be real with you, I ain't gonna never be no saint. I'm gonna fuck up now and a lot more later. I'm spoiled, rich and use to getting any bitch I want. But, what I want right now is you, Monie. And if you can deal with the uncertainty that who I might be tomorrow may be different than who I am today, than I'm yours. You got my heart, Monie. I just hope that's enough for you. For now anyway."

Monie tried to hide her excitement. "So what you saying, C?"

"I'm asking will you be my lady?" He shook his head. "Got me sounding like some corny-ass-R&B-type nigga and shit. You know what I'm saying. Will you be my bitch?"

Monie answered him with a sloppy ass kiss. Then she separated from him and said, "You know I will."

C pulled her toward him, gripped her meaty ass cheeks, and kissed her harder. "If you woulda said no, I was gonna fuck you up," he laughed.

"Since we got that out of the way, now won't we go get my clothes from the dry cleaner," Monie said.

"That was what you were about to do?" C laughed. "You looking like you bout to hit the club, and shit. Got my head all fucked up thinking you was rolling with another nigga."

"Naw, that was it," Monie giggled. "It's the last day I can have it in there, and I don't want them giving my shit away."

"You wild as shit, but that's why I love you."

C and Monie just paid for her dry cleaning. C was holding the bags and they were on their way out of the store, when Oscar and Persia strolled inside.

"Well, well, well," Persia said rubbing her pregnant belly. "If it isn't Mister and Misses Camelot. I never been this close to royalty before. I mean can I have an autograph?"

"We don't have no time for this shit," C said walking around her.

Monie was right at his side, clutching his hand.

"I see you lost a little weight, bitch," Persia said, trying her best to start a fight she couldn't win.

"Glad you noticed," Monie responded.

Monie could've cracked her limbs, but it wasn't worth it. Besides Persia was pregnant, and Monie had C. The battle had been won and in a twist, the fat girl got the boy.

"What you mean you don't have no time for this shit?" Oscar said to C, as if he just remembered what C said. "So you can fuck her, but you can't do right by her in the streets?"

"Main Man, you don't know shit about me," C said to him. "You keep letting your girl fill you up

with Heart Juice, and you gonna get your feelings hurt in a minute. Now back off."

"Me get my feelings hurt," Oscar laughed touching his chest. "You and what army?"

"Let's bounce, baby," C said kissing Monie on the neck. He was treating them like two flies around the picnic table. "We ain't got time for no Wangstas. I'm trying to go to our house and dig that pussy out."

When Persia saw C kiss Monie on the neck, and heard his comment, she started ticking like a bomb. All of the pain, the hurt and the rejection she felt all of her young life came flooding out of her pores. While most people felt bitterness on an inconsistent basis, Persia's heart was jealous the majority of the time, making it difficult for her to make rational decisions.

So when they walked closer to their car she whispered in Oscar's ear, "Did you hear what he just said? He said fuck your mother," she lied.

Oscar's chest swole up, and he immediately stepped to C who had just closed the door for Monie, and was walking around to the driver's side.

"What you just say?" Oscar asked, his glasses steamy. "About my mother?"

C laughed at him, "So what, your girl lying to you again?" C moved to open his car door, until Oscar, who was moving his hands too wildly, accidently-brushed C's cheek with his index finger.

In a second flat, C put the nigga on his back like a throw rug. His navy glasses crashed against his nose, and C stomped them. To make matters worse, C beat him like a clump of bread dough. C kicked him in the chin, neck, solar plexus, and everywhere else his black and silver Foamposites would land.

He didn't stop whipping his ass until Oscar said, "Mercy. Mercy."

With those words C bent down and looked at him. "That's the last time I'll be so lenient. If you come for me or my girl again, I'll kill you."

C grabbed the car door, and pulled it open. Persia could hear Monie laughing hysterically from the inside. This did nothing but ignite Persia's fire.

When C pulled off Persia looked down at Oscar. In her opinion he looked quite bazaar, and she certainly didn't want to be promised as his wife anymore. But first she needed him for revenge.

"You know what you gotta do when you get up from taking that nap don't you?"

"No," he said coughing up blood. "What?"

"You gotta call your mother. Wake up, boy, C just declared war."

CHAPTER 23
KAREN

Karen was sitting in her office going over the financials for the Klan. Ever since she learned that she was HIV positive, which she kept to herself, she was not feeling well. Although she could've gone to the doctors, and got prescribed a cocktail to keep her disease at bay, she didn't want too. She couldn't risk one of the members seeing the medications, and alerting the other members. Instead she decided to abstain from sex, and make sure the Black Water Klan was financially stable in the event of her demise, so that Oscar, the next leader, would be okay.

She just finished running the numbers when Oscar, Persia, Roman and Lance rushed into her office. Roman and Lance didn't know what was going on, but when they saw Oscar's face, they became concerned and followed them.

"Ma, a war has started," Oscar said to her, from the other side of the desk. His cracked glasses made him look eerie.

Karen leaped up from her seat, ran around the desk and sprinted up to Oscar. She observed his bruised face, and the spaces where his teeth use to be in his mouth.

"Son, what has happened to you?" She removed his fractured glasses. "Who did this?"

"Persia and I were walking out of the compound, when C, and other members of the Emerald City Squad ran up to us. They jumped me, and said that there will be more where this was coming from. Other members will receive the same punishment."

Oscar remembered all of the words Persia gave him to recite, just like a good little parakeet should.

Karen stepped back, and sat on the edge of her desk. "But this doesn't make any sense."

"It sure doesn't," Lance said. "Something sounds off." He smelled something foul, but would keep his ideas of what was really going on to himself. "Way off."

"Why would they do that, when they know we have Persia?" Karen inquired.

"Because they don't care about me anymore," Persia said walking up to her. "They want to rid the world of the Klan all together. We gotta do something, Ms. Karen. Before they get us."

"You don't care about your own people? And what we could do to them?"

"It's not my concern anymore," Persia said. "This family is."

Karen didn't trust the girl. But still, with her own eyes she could see that her son had been attacked. She felt dumb for trusting Carissa and her crew, and now she wanted blood. They could keep the money.

Karen walked back around her desk, and picked up the phone. She dialed a number, and waited a second. "Yes, Carissa, this is Karen. You wanted a war, well you got one."

CHAPTER 24
CARISSA

I'm driving one of Toi's cars, on the way to find Persia. Nobody knew I was coming alone to find her, but I didn't care. Besides, Mercedes' left Toi's house to take care of personal business, and Yvette was in the house watching Treasure for me. Observing Yvette with Treasure is like watching a robot with a child. She seemed so unnatural and she isn't maternal at all. But, she did it for me and that's all that matters.

At first, I was confused when I got the call from Karen. I mean, how could I have started a war with her, when I had been hiding out and trying to save my own life? None of this made sense, but I'm sure my lying daughter was behind it all.

While driving down the street, I was about to lose my mind when I saw Persia walking up the sidewalk, a few blocks from the compound. I pulled the car over and said, "Persia, come here."

Persia bent down, looked into the car, and kept it moving. I pulled back up on her, jumped out and snatched her by the neck. At this moment I could care less that she's pregnant, and getting ready to drop this baby any minute. I stuff her into the passenger seat of the car, and when she tries to get out, I give her a stiff boot to the forehead, push her back inside, and slam the car door.

When I jog to my door, a man walking on the sidewalk says, "Hey, lady, you can't do that. She's pregnant."

I pull my gun on him and say, "You wanna try me?"

He runs off in the other direction, and I get behind the wheel of the car and speed away from the scene. I'm so mad now I'm crying, and I have yet to say anything to Persia.

"Mommy, you're scaring me," Persia says softly. She wipes my dusty boot print off her head.

I don't respond, I just move the car in and out of traffic like I'm on a racetrack. I'm tired of this little girl hurting my feelings. I'm tired of her talking to me in any kind of way. And more than it all, I'm tired of her not loving me. No I wasn't the best mother in the world. And no I didn't always give her my love, but I want to make good on that now, but she won't allow me.

"I hate you," she says to me folding her arms over her belly.

"Tell me something I don't know," I say driving faster.

"You forgot my 12th birthday, mommy. How could you?"

"What are you talking about?" I say. "I ain't never forgot not one of your birthdays. You sound like a fool."

"You forgot it, mommy," she says softer. "You didn't remember."

As she continues to lie, I pull up all of her birthdays in my mind. On her fifth birthday we had a party for her at Kings Dominion. On the sixth birthday, we had a party for her at Disney World. The seventh, eighth and ninth birthdays, we had one in Emerald city, so we could be close to our drug operation. On the tenth birthday, one of Lavelle's best friends was murdered in Texas, so we had her party at a community center in Houston. It was real nice too, because we bought a balloon bounce and everything, and Persia made a lot of new friends. On the eleventh birthday, me and Lavelle got into a fight, so we had a small party in our apartment in Emerald City. On the twelfth birthday we, on the twelfth birthday we…we…uh…we…

I pull the car over and look at her. "We had a party, Persia, I know we did."

"Nothing," she says softly with tears running down her face. "You forgot."

"But there was a cake. A cake was there, remember," I ask. "It was pink and you got your first purse too."

"Daddy bought that cake for me," she pouts. "And my purse. Not you. You forgot."

Warm tears stream down my face, and fall into the crease of my breasts. I turn toward her, and grip her hands into mine. They are soft, like they were when she was a little girl, and we'd stay up all night playing Patty Cake.

I look deep into her eyes, and with everything I say, "I'm sorry. I'm so sorry, Persia. I was the kind of mother I despise, and you didn't deserve that when you were growing up. You didn't deserve any of it. I was wrong, and I will never forgive myself. But you tell me how I can repair our bond, and on my life I will do it. I'll do anything you say, you just gotta let me know."

"It's too late," she mumbles.

"It's never too late," I say gripping her hands tightly. "Don't say that."

"I don't love you anymore," she says.

My heart pumps wildly. Like it wants to fly out of my chest. "I can't deal with that, Persia. I can't deal with you not loving me. I can't deal with you not being in my life. I'm lost without my girls, don't you see? Fuck the money, fuck the drugs, and fuck everything else."

She looks at me and rolls her eyes. "So you admit to doing drugs now?"

"Yes," I say. "But, I'm done with that shit. I made a mess of my life and in turn, I made a mess of you and your sister's lives too. But I'm going to do better now, Persia. You just tell me what to do."

"Anything?" She says with wide eyes.

"Anything."

"Help me get with C," she pleads. "Help me show him I can be a better girlfriend than Monie. Please, mommy."

I feel deflated. Like I'm a balloon, and someone just popped me with a shiny stickpin. "Persia, C's heart is not mine to provide. I'm sorry. But, he has moved on with his life. Now I know C, and I know he'll be a great father to your child. That much I can be sure of. I also know that I'll love my grandbaby with everything I have, and Mercedes will too."

"Mercedes?" she frowns. "She not coming near my baby."

"Persia, let's talk about all of that later," I say. I don't want to make her too mad when I gotta take her out of here.

"No, let's talk about it now," she says. "If I can't have C, Mercedes will never see my baby," she screams in my face. "Do you hear me? Never!" She pushes the car door open and dips into the neighborhood.

I'm about to chase her, but she leaves her purse behind. I go into it, and pull out about ten pages of a Xeroxed document. The document looks handwritten, and I'm immediately curious. I read the 50th Commandment out loud.

"Thou shall follow thy leader, always."

What the fuck type of shit is this? As I go through the document, most of the lines read the same way. Some commandments are weirder than others, and I'm worried more for my daughter's life.

I gotta get her out of there and I gotta do it now!

CHAPTER 25
YVETTE

When Carissa comes back with the doctrine that she'd gotten from Persia, and I scan through it, I'm blown away. I'm sitting on the edge of one of the twin beds looking at Carissa, who is sitting on the other mattress directly across from me.

"What kind of shit is this?" I ask holding the papers.

"Exactly," she says.

"Take this bullshit back," I hand them back to her. "What do you want to do about this, Carissa? We in a fucked up position now, with not a lot of freedom, or authority."

"I know," she cries. "But I gotta get my baby out of there, Yvette. She's not about this life. She'll die in there."

I sigh. I'm not going to lie, Persia is getting on my last nerves, and I don't have no more space in my heart for her. I mean, why she gotta be giving her mother the blues all of the time? This poor girl haven't had a break since never. Still, Carissa's pain is mine. She's my sister, so we have to do something.

"So what do you want to do?"

"Pay her off," Carissa says.

I stand up and walk across the room. "I thought she said she didn't want money?"

"They always want money," she responds.

"Carissa, we don't hardly have no money right now. Do you remember, everything we owned is gone?"

"I know, and the fucked up part is I'll need what little money we got," she says.

My eyes widen. "You need it all?" I laugh. "I just told you that we can't afford to be giving that bitch none of our paper, and you tell me you want it all? Carissa, you not thinking straight." I hit the top of my head with my knuckles. "I know you want your daughter back, but you gonna put us in the dog house to get her? Is that smart?"

"We'll get more money."

"News flash, sweetie, we need money to make money," I say. "If you take it all we assed out. I'm talking about no ends."

She sighs. "Will you help me out or not? That's all that matters."

Fuck! This is the worst time for her to be pulling the friend card. Yes I want to be there for her, but why it gotta be like this?

"Okay," I moan.

"Okay what?" she smiles.

"Okay I'll give you what I got," I respond. "But you gotta ask Mercedes for hers when she gets here. She's still out on business."

Carissa grins like a happy kid, and pulls out her phone. “I’ll call Karen now. Maybe I can meet up with her and give her the money for Persia tonight.”

“You mean we,” I tell her. “I’m not letting you go nowhere by yourself. Fuck that. I don’t trust my foul-ass sister.”

I walk back towards her, and sit on the bed across from her. She dials the number, places the call on speaker, and Karen answers. I can’t believe my sister Karen is being such an evil bitch, and I wonder how our lives would’ve been if we grew up together. I guess we will never know.

“Karen, this is Carissa.”

“I know who you are,” Karen responds dryly.

Carissa clears her throat. “Is my daughter with you?”

“She is.”

“Good, because I wanted to talk to you about an offer.”

“I’m listening.”

“As it stands now, my daughter is brainwashed by you and your organization.”

Karen sighs.

“But, I want my family back. Now I’m willing to give you the last fifty I owe you, plus fifty more if you relinquish Persia to me now.”

Karen starts laughing. “What’s so funny?” Carissa asks her.

“I don’t want your money, Carissa, I want your life.”

“What the fuck you just say,” I yell to my sister.

"Hello, Yvette. Funny talking to you again."

"What did you just say to my friend, bitch?" I yell.

"I think I made myself clear," Karen responds. "Now you and your friends have killed two of our leaders, Black Water and Tamir. And just recently you have beaten my son to every inch of his life. So I'm saying that you wanted war, and now you have one."

"Tamir and Black Water's lives are on us, but they were coming for us, Karen," I tell her. "We had to defend ourselves. But your son's punishment is not our doing. You are barking up the wrong tree."

"Stop lying, Yvette," Karen yells. "Unlike your friends, I am not amused by your words. My son was beaten savagely and he almost died today. Not to mention I am aware that Mercedes wanted war with us. A conversation was overheard by one of our members, so I know it is true. Don't bother lying."

"Where did you get your tales from?" I ask.

"Persia."

Carissa's eyes widen, and pain spreads all over her face.

I'm equally as devastated. I mean I know Persia was doing the most over there, to get at C, but I never thought she would go this far. She's staging a war, just because she can't get who and what she wants.

"I love my niece, but she's lying to you," I say.

"We'll talk about who's lying on who, after blood is drawn," she says. "I'll be in contact."

"Not if we get to you first," I say.

CHAPTER 26

MERCEDES

"Well what do you want," Mercedes questioned. "Because whatever you want I can give it to you. I'm a very wealthy woman, Karen. And, I can give you anything your heart desires. Just speak on it."

Karen laughed. "It's just like you bitches to think everything is about money. What I want runs much deeper than monetary value."

"I'll give you whatever you're asking," Mercedes said. "Just say the word."

"I want salvation," her wild eyes looked into Mercedes'. "Can you give me salvation for abandoning one of my commandments? If you can't, this baby can give me salvation with his life."

Mercedes paused a few moments to consider the question. She knew that Karen, and the rest of the Black Water Klan members, were brainwashed into believing Black Water's fake doctrine. Black Water had mind-fucked the Klan so long that they believed everything he said. So if she wanted to get through to her, she had to think smartly.

"Karen, I don't know what you mean by salvation," Mercedes started. "But, I will give you my life if you don't hurt my grandbaby. Please."

Karen looked into Mercedes' eyes, smiled, and jumped off of the Woodrow Wilson Bridge, with the baby in her arms.

"Oh my, God," I yell waking up from a nightmare. My face is completely wet with sweat.

"You're okay," Jackson says sitting up next to me in his bed. "You're with me, in my house and you're safe." He wipes my face with his big hand.

I look at his brown face, and place my hand against his warm cheek. My fingers rub over his silky goatee. "I'm so sorry," I say to him. "I'm supposed to be over here spending time with you, and here I am, taking a nap and having nightmares. I'm so embarrassed."

"Mercedes, this ain't nothing," he sits up and leans against the black headboard. He pulls me toward him, and I lay my face against his hairy muscular chest. "I love that you are here with me. Don't worry about the small shit."

"Even though it will hurt your brother? That you and I are together?"

He laughs. "Like I told you before, Mercedes, my brother isn't that type of nigga. We good, trust me."

"I know you said that, but I never understood what you meant by it. He seemed really attached to me."

"For starters my brother is a male stripper. He is use to meeting women, seducing them and then taking their money. And if you ask me, he is great at what he does. He hasn't had a real job in fifteen years."

I laugh. "Well he had the hookup with me, because I was outright paying him for his services too. But, that arrangement was my idea, not his."

"He told me," he says. "But when I saw you, I couldn't believe how beautiful you were. Most of the women he ropes are overweight, insecure and lonely. I knew the moment I looked into your eyes that you weren't that kind of girl. So it was strange to actually meet you." He runs his fingers through my hair. "I'm glad I stole you from Lloyd, my brother ain't nothing but an identity thief anyway. He been done went through your personal records, and milked you for every bone you had."

I sit up and look into his eyes. "W-what y-you mean milk me for every bone?" I stutter.

"That's what he does, Mercedes," he laughs. "He'll find a rich prospect, get her personal information, and drain her bank accounts. As a matter of fact, he must've made a big come up, because he caught a plane to the Cayman Islands the other day, and told the family that he ain't never coming back."

I'm shaking so hard my teeth are rattling. This can't be true, please God don't tell me I allowed a nigga to come into my house and rob me and my friend's blind. The worst part about it is Toi told me to get rid of the nigga, and I didn't listen. Please, God don't let it be so.

"Jackson, can you get a hold of him now?" I ask touching his hand.

"Sure, baby," he says. "But what's wrong?"

"Please just call him for me."

"What you want me to say?"

"Do you have the kind of relationship with him, where he'll keep shit real with you?" I feel like I'm about to pass out.

"If by real you mean brag, I'll say yes."

"Then call him for me and ask him about his last hit," I beg.

"Mercedes—,"

"Jackson, please," I plead with him squeezing his hand. "For me."

Jackson picks up the cell phone on his nightstand. "Okay, but don't say anything, otherwise he'll know you are here and lie."

"I won't say a word," I swear placing my hand over my heart. "I promise."

Jackson dials a number. I watch each number he selects, and store it in my mental database for later. He places the call on speaker and it rings. When I hear Lloyd's voice come through the phone, I'm heated.

"What up, nigga," Jackson says on the phone. "Let me find out you struck it big, and you ain't take your big brother with you. I thought we were boys?"

"You know how I do," Lloyd brags. "I be on the move and making moves. And you thought there wasn't no money in stripping."

"Well the family saying you hit pay dirt this time," Jackson says looking at me with sad eyes. He probably finally gets what's going on, that his brother took me for my paper.

"Yes, nigga, but this is the big one, I'm officially a millionaire."

The room is spinning. "Word?"

"Yes, remember that bitch Mercedes that was tricking off on me," he says, "well I went through her shit when I was there a few days ago, and found some paper work for some overseas accounts. Nigga, why I call my man at the bank, who flipped the money into accounts in my name? I never would've guessed this broad would be worth that much money. The thing is you know its drug money too, so she ain't saying shit about it."

"Word?" Jackson says rubbing my leg.

"Word, nigga," Lloyd laughs. "I'm out the game now. I'm about to open up some beachfront properties and everything, and sit good for the rest of my life. You and the family welcome to come join me. I'm living large."

Jackson hangs up. I guess he can't take it anymore.

I'm so pathetic I wish I could punch myself in the face. I let him into my home, to rob me and steal from me. That nigga wasn't no slave, he was a thief, and a good one at that.

The phone rings again, but Jackson turns it off. "Baby, I'm so sorry," he says to me. "He got you?"

"Yes," I say dryly.

"So what are you going to do?"

"Nothing," I lie.

"Nothing?" he asks leaning in. "I mean, is it true? That he got that much money off of you?"

Before answering I think of my current situation. Part of me is relieved. At first I thought the Feds hit us up, and seized our accounts. But now that I know its Lloyd, I know how to play the situation. I'm looking at Lloyd as my personal bank for the time being. I'll let him think he's good for a minute, and then go get what's mine.

"It's true," I say. "He got me for some money, but it ain't all the money he talking about neither. If it's more than fifty thousand I would be guessing."

"Whoa," he says like he's relieved. "I thought I was gonna have to call somebody to snatch his ass off of the islands. I'm glad it's light money and you'll be okay though."

Wow. That comment Jackson makes, about sending somebody to snatch him up, causes me to get a little wet down low. Knowing that he would go that far for me makes me think I have a keeper on my hands.

"Jackson, you mind if I make a call real quick."

"Go 'head, bay, I'll be in here waiting on you."

"Thanks," I smile.

I snatch my cell phone from my purse, hop off of the bed, and dip into the bathroom. I close the door behind me and call one of my soldiers in Emerald City. I have to see what's going on, to make things make sense. I get one of them on the phone in ten seconds.

"Knight, how are things looking in Emerald?"

"You ain't hear?"

"Hear what?"

"Some white man who owns *National Improvement* for a *Greater Generation Association* has bought Emerald City and Camelot. But niggas around here call his company *NIGGA* since those are the main letters in his company. He tearing Emerald and Camelot down and building expensive condos, in the next few weeks. You know how they doing with all of these properties in D.C. Niggas gonna have to live in outer space now to find cheap rent prices."

My jaw drops. What do you know, Judah's indictment didn't have nothing to do with Emerald and Camelot. "So that's why all of the suits have been around Camelot and Emerald? For some real estate deal?"

"Yep," he sighs. "After all these years, and all the money, it's finally over, boss. What we gonna do now?"

Silence.

"Boss. What we gonna do?"

CHAPTER 27
CARISSA

My jaw still hurts from when Yvette stole me in the face, after I told her I was meeting Persia by myself. But, I didn't want her coming along, and saying the wrong thing to upset my daughter. I swear me and my friends are much too physical with each other. That shit is gonna have to change too. The fights we had would've ended most friendships along time ago. I guess that's why our shit is real.

I'm driving in my car on the way to meet Persia. Earlier tonight she called me to say she wanted to meet me alone. She said she wanted to apologize for how she treated me, when we were in the car. I told her I wanted to talk to her too, about the papers I found in her purse. She said she would answer any questions I had, and I hoped that was true.

When I pull up at Mama's Kitchen, and step out, I see Lil C running up to me. I jog toward him thinking something is wrong. I leave my car door open, and my purse inside. But I'm worried, because C looks like he's seen the devil and his energy frightens me.

"Aunt Carissa, you gotta get out of here while you still can," he says to me. "And you gotta tell ma and them to stay low." He keeps looking around. "We followed Karen and them here, and they must be waiting to meet you."

"C, what you mean? I mean, what's going on? I'm supposed to meet Persia tonight."

"I can't talk in detail right now," he says. "But tell my mother I love her, and if I make it out of this shit alive, we gonna start all over, and put the bad stuff behind us."

Tears roll down my face. "C, I swear to God you're scaring me. Talk to me, baby. Maybe we can help you."

"Don't be scared," he continues. "And no matter what, I want you to know you're a good fucking mother. You hear what I'm saying? You a good mother, Aunt Carissa, and I can see the love in your eyes when you look at Persia. Remember that. Try not to take the shit that is getting ready to happen on your heart. Persia is confused. Now get the fuck outta here while you still can."

I'm about to run, when I see Oscar and Karen get out of a white box van. Persia is right next to them, and she's grinning. Then this girl does something that breaks my heart into more pieces. She throws a fuck you finger up in the air, and sticks out her tongue. She does this shit to me. Her own mother.

"Get the fuck out of here," C yells, pushing me to the ground. "Now."

Out of nowhere, a dude in another car snatches C up off of his feet, and pulls him into a truck. I get up, and take off running to try to get to my purse and gun, in the car. I gotta help C.

I make it there, but C is gone and bullets ring out in my direction. I slam the car door, and a bullet fractures the drivers' side window.

I get inside, step on the gas and push forward. A man who is aiming a gun at me, fires into the window again, and misses my head by inches. I press on the gas harder, and crash into him. He bounces on the hood of the car, and rolls off.

More bullets hit the car, but I don't look back. I make it out of there with my life in tow.

Two thoughts occupy my mind at this moment. One, that C tried to save my life, and two that my daughter tried to take it.

CHAPTER 28

TOI

Toi was in the bed with her boyfriend Michael watching porn. She had a blunt in one hand, and the remote control in the other, while she fast-forwarded trying to find her favorite part of the movie.

"Baby, stop fucking around already," Mike said stroking his dick. "You got me ready to bang that juicy pussy out. Now hit play, and lets get it on."

"Stop, Mike, you know I like to watch my favorite part when we fuck."

"Man, ain't nobody trying to bone you, while you look at fifteen inches of another nigga's dick."

"Thirteen inches," Toi corrects him. "Sir Hungs-A-Lot has the biggest dick in the world, and you know I love watching them bitches take it. Do you know how big a bitch's snatch gotta be to handle that much meat?"

"Damn, my bitch a freak," Michael says.

"And you love me for it too," she says pushing him playfully.

He grins. "You already know I do."

They were just about to get it in when Toi's phone rung. She picked it up from the end table, and answered. "Hello."

"Toi, this Carissa. Where you at?"

"I'm at my apartment out Maryland," Toi said, catching the anxiousness in her voice. "Where you? At my house?"

"No, I'm on my way to the Compound. Please call my friends until you get a hold of them. I can't get Yvette or Mercedes on the phone. C has been kidnapped, and I need help."

Toi hopped out of bed and begin putting on her clothes. "Where the fuck is this Compound? Where we first saw Persia?"

"Yes, and please find them for me, girl. I don't know what else to do. If something happens to C, Mercedes will die, and I will too. Karen just called me, so I'm going to try and handle business."

"Alone?"

"I don't have a choice. Just call my friends...please."

"I'm on it!"

CHAPTER 29
KAREN

Karen stood in front of the wall and looked down at her hostages. Behind her were Oscar, Roman, and Lance. Oscar was wiping blood from his knuckles, due to the beat down they'd just performed on C, while Lance stood watching and cleaning his nails with a knife.

"Ms. Karen, I don't know why you're doing this to me," Persia said as she looked up at her. "I'm on your side. I'm a member of the Klan. Remember? I'm loyal to you."

"You're loyal to no one," Karen replied.

Karen looked down at Persia and Lil C who were tied in chairs that were back to back. They were in the basement of the main building in the compound.

Earlier that day Karen placed a call to Carissa, to tell her she was waiting for her there. She also told her to bring the money, or her daughter would die. But, that was only one part of Karen's plan. Her sick mind had something else in play. She wanted Carissa to tear her friend's heart apart.

"What do you have to say for yourself," Karen asked C. "For what you and your friends did to my son?"

"Nothing," he said spitting out blood. "I ain't got shit to say."

Roman, Lance and Oscar had beat C so badly, while C's hands were tied behind his back, that C lost a lot of blood and a few teeth too.

"There's gotta be something you want to say for yourself," Karen said to C.

"Unless you gonna untie me, and let me go at that pussy nigga Oscar one on one, I don't have shit to say."

"Fuck you nigga, you jumped me the last time, that's the only reason you got the best of me," Oscar lied.

"Bitch, I beat your ass straight up," C corrected him. "You can lie to these other niggas if you want too, but, you and me know the truth. I turned your glasses into sand."

"But why am I tied up?" Persia asked selfishly. "I'm not involved in any of this shit. I even called my mother like you asked, and lead her to the restaurant. I'm on your side."

"You're tied up because Roman and Lance told me that they saw you coming out of my office. That means I can't trust you. Truthfully, I never trusted you," Karen responded. "But my son was in love and couldn't see straight. I knew it was dangerous keeping a member of the Emerald City Squad in our compound, but you were disloyal to your family, and

the business relationship with them proved to be beneficial for us at the time. Now my need for you is over."

"Please don't kill me," Persia cried. "I'm too young to die."

"I'm not going to kill you," Karen smiled. "I'm going to give your mother an option, she can't refuse."

Before Persia could respond, two Black Water Klan members brought Carissa into the basement. They pushed her inside of the room. "Here is the money," Carissa said tossing the bag on the floor, with one hundred thousand dollars inside. "It's all there. Now let my family go."

"Sorry, but that is not how things are going down tonight," Karen said. "I control this show not you."

"Then how are things going down?" Carissa asked. "I did what you asked. The money is all there. Count it."

"You must choose who lives or dies today."

"Choose?" Carissa frowned. "What are you talking about? You got the money so I want both of them. That was the deal."

"And I said it doesn't work like that. You have to choose who to save, and who to die. You can save your daughter or your nephew if you like, but the choice is yours."

"Oh my God, please don't make me do this," Carissa begged. "You can't be serious."

"I'm deathly serious," Karen replied. "You know what, I was once a part of such a vicious option like this when I was a child. But guess what, my mother chose Yvette over me." She laughed. "And I was thrown on the streets like a bag of trash, like I didn't matter."

"But both of these aren't my kids," Carissa said. "He's my nephew and this is my daughter. It isn't the same thing. Please don't make me do this."

"I know who the fuck they are to you," Karen yelled. "And again I tell you, that you must choose."

"Mommy, what are you waiting on? I'm your daughter," Persia said. "I love you. So tell her you want me to get out of here, so they can let me go. Fuck, C!"

"Aunt Carissa, it's okay," C said. "Choose Persia over me. That way my baby will be safe. I'm not going to feel any kind of way, or make you feel guilty for deciding. I just want this shit over with, and I want my child safe. It's fine, just get them out of here."

"You see," Persia said. "He said let me go. So tell her, ma. I want to get my baby out of here too. You gotta choose me because I'm pregnant."

"Oh no," Karen said. "Even if she chooses you, the baby stays here with me."

"What?" Carissa cried. "But, why? This baby isn't even your blood."

"I don't care about this baby," Persia said. "Fuck this baby! Just pick me, mommy."

"Karen, you can't have my grandchild," Carissa screamed. "I can't leave the baby behind. The baby isn't yours."

"But I'll raise it like mine," Karen laughed. "You see, either way you lose."

Carissa dropped to her knees and sobbed uncontrollably. When she was done she reached in her back pocket. Oscar was about to shoot her thinking she had a weapon until she said, "I'm unarmed. Your man took my gun before he let me come down here. I just want to read you something, Karen. Please." She looked at Karen. "May I?"

Karen studied her for a minute. It wasn't like anything she said would influence Karen's decision, but it was interesting to see Carissa perform. "Go ahead."

Carissa pulled the folded doctrine paper from her pocket. She opened it up and read it out loud. "The 80th Commandment. The mother of a dying child must always be granted two wishes. And these wishes, no matter what, can not be denied."

Karen's eyes widened. "Where did you get that from?" She snatched the sheet from her hand. "Who gave this to you?"

"It doesn't matter," Carissa said not wanting to throw her child under the bus. "But this is your word, not mine."

"But you can't...I can't..."

"Mother, you don't have to honor this commandment," Oscar said walking up behind her. "Black Water wrote that for our people," Oscar

clarified. "He did it so if one of our members lost a child during the a war, they would get some sort of reward. It's not for outsiders."

"But he didn't specify in the commandment," Karen said under her breath looking at the papers. She observed Carissa. "I'll honor this, because I'm righteous. But you smoothed over one important fact. For me to honor this, you must have a dying child, which means you can not save Persia with one of your wishes."

"I know," Carissa sobbed. "Oh my, God, I know."

"Mommy, what's going on?" Persia asked with wide eyes. "What is she talking about?"

Karen suddenly grinned. "So you are prepared to sacrifice your own child, to save another?"

"I don't have a choice."

"Then what are your wishes?"

"That you free C, and that I am allowed to take my grandchild with me."

Karen was shocked. "But the child isn't born yet."

Carissa looked at Persia. "I know."

Persia let out a blood-curdling scream. "Mommy no," she shook her head. "No, mommy, you can't do this to me. Please."

Karen snatched the knife from Lance's hand that he was using to clean his nails. She walked up to Carissa and said, "If you want the child that badly," she handed her the knife, "then you take it out yourself."

CHAPTER 30
MERCEDES

"You driving too slow is all I'm saying," I yell at Yvette from the passenger seat. "Press the gas on this bitch!"

"Mercedes, I'm pushing the limit on this girl's car already," Yvette tells me. "I don't even know why she would have a Prius in her garage anyway. Who the fuck drives around in one of these little mothafuckas?"

"I guess somebody who likes to stay low key like Toi," I yell. "And thanks to you, your car was out of gas, so we didn't have no choice. Just be glad she had another ride in her garage."

When I found out that C had been kidnapped, I felt my world had been switched with a less fortunate bitch. I'm having the worst luck of my life, but when I was in the bathroom, I prayed for some better days. Hopefully God likes me, and will honor my prayers.

So much is going on, that I didn't have time to tell Yvette about Emerald and Camelot being bought by some white man, or that I knew who had our money. I was too embarrassed to tell her the last part anyway, and planned to hold off on that info until I could get my hands on Lloyd, and our cash.

"Ain't that them right there?" Yvette says to me when we pull up in front of the main building. "Ain't that C and Carissa?"

A smile spreads across my face. "Yes it is, Yvette, and it looks like they got the baby too."

"But where is Persia?" she asks.

Yvette pulls the tiny little white car in front of the building, and we jump out. C doesn't have on a shirt, because it's wrapped around the baby. I run straight for C and surprisingly, he hugs me tightly into his arms. I cry as he holds me, this is what I always wanted.

I pull away from him and say, "C, I'm so sorry about all of the shit I did to you, I really am," I wipe my hands over the sides of his face. "I should've been straight up with you about your father, and that was my mistake. I took a sucker's way out, and I hope you can forgive me. Or will at least try."

"Ma, let's talk about it later," he says.

"Wait a minute," I say noticing his bruised face, "who did this shit to you? And are you missing teeth?"

"It don't even matter, we just gotta get out of here," he tells me. "Before something else happens."

Just when he says that four large Hummers pull up in front of the compound. My heart rate increases, because I know these are members of the Klan. We are dead now.

"Please say you're strapped," I ask Yvette. "Please tell me you are."

"For the first time in my life I'm not," Yvette sighs.

"Me either," Carissa said with the baby in her arms.

My heart drops with the news. A tall man wearing fatigues jumps out of the first Hummer and approaches us. C squares up with the hands, preparing to use the only weapons he has to defend us, his fists. But instead of hurting us the man says, "I'm Sarge, Bambi sent us."

Now I see the girl Race, who I saw earlier at Toi's house, get out one of the other Hummers. She looks up at the two Black Water Klan buildings. "The rest of them in there?" she asks me. "The Klan members?"

"Yes."

She cocks her weapon and says, "Not anymore." She goes inside, followed by what looked like twenty men.

"Ya'll get out of here," Sarge tells us. "The Pretty Kings sent us, and not to sound melodramatic or nothing, but we got it from here."

He didn't have to tell us twice. Me, Yvette, Carissa, C and the new baby pile inside the tiny car.

When I hear Carissa sobbing in the back seat I ask, "Where is Persia?"

"We can't talk about it now, ma," C says to me. "I'll put you down with that later. Leave Carissa be."

If she isn't here it means she's dead and I love it.

It's quiet for a few more moments. I think about the Pretty Kings, and how they looked out for us. I don't know what this act will cost us, and even more, I don't know if we can afford it. Even still, I'm grateful. Grateful that my son, my grandbaby, and my friends are alive, and we are all together.

When I look over at Yvette, I notice that she seems like she's in her head. "What you thinking about, Yvette?" I ask her.

"That we use to command an army like that," she says under her breath. "I guess our reign is over now."

EPILOGUE
ONE MONTH LATER

Yvette, Mercedes, Carissa, C, Treasure, Chante and Jackson were in the park with the grandbaby having a picnic. Although Yvette and Carissa were broke, unsure of their futures and helpless, Mercedes was on cloud nine. She was in a loving relationship with Jackson, and had won the love of C, and Chante again. Carissa, on the other hand, wasn't so lucky.

Carissa was sitting on the wooden bench in the park, looking at Mercedes rock the baby in her arms. C was over her right shoulder, playing with the baby's foot. Chante was on the other side of Mercedes, cooing at her new nephew. Jackson was behind Mercedes, with his hands on her waist, looking over her head at the beautiful child dressed in a peach sailor's suit. Treasure was across the park talking to a little boy, being very fresh.

Holding a beer, Yvette walked over to Carissa on the bench, and sat next to her. "What's on your mind?" Yvette asked her.

"Have you ever noticed that Mercedes always gets to have it all?" Carissa said looking at the hap-

py family. "Here it is, me and you are broke, living in her friend Toi's house, and fighting with each other every other day, but Mercedes is living with Jackson, with C, Chante and the baby, playing house. Why is it that luck always seems to follow her around? When am I going to roll sevens, huh? When do I get to win the game? Why I gotta always roll craps?"

Yvette sighed. "Look, Mercedes isn't always lucky, she just makes the best out of the breaks she gets that's all. If you ask me, we should start doing the same thing."

Carissa looked at Yvette. Her eyebrows pulled closely together. "Do you know that every time I hold my grandbaby in my arms, it cries like I'm pinching it?"

"Carissa, it's just a baby. It don't—"

"It doesn't like me," Carissa yelled. "The baby don't like me, because she telling it not to like me."

"You sound like a fucking fool," Yvette screamed.

Mercedes turned around and said, "Ya'll okay? What ya'll fussing about now?"

"We just peachy, 'Cedes," Carissa said sarcastically. "Everything is just as peachy as that faggoted sailor's suit you bought for Ryan."

Mercedes rolled her eyes, turned around, and joined her family again with the baby.

"Carissa, just what the fuck are you getting at?" Yvette whispered heavily. "Because I'm not feeling

the heat rising off of you. It stinks and you need to check yourself."

"I'm saying that I gave my daughter's life for her son's and Ryan, and the baby don't want to have nothing to do with me. I'm saying that I have nightmares— every time I close my eyes, about the basement cesarean that I had to give my oldest daughter. And I'm saying that it seems that Mercedes' life goes along, untouched, just like Persia always told me before I killed her."

Yvette drank all of her beer, and slammed it on the table. "You a rotten, bitch, Carissa. Just as rotten as a brown apple can be."

"Me?" Carissa pointed to herself.

"Yeah you, bitch. You sitting over here, in your fucked up attitude like you the only one thinking about what happened to Persia. We love you, so we feel that shit too, skank! Not to mention that I spent two hours on the phone with Mercedes last night, trying to come up with some way to cheer you up. Talking about she can't sleep because she understands how much you sacrificed for her, C and the baby. Don't read a book if you not gonna understand what it means, bitch. That girl is fucked up, Carissa. Real fucked up. And so what if she gets a little love along the way? Who gives a fuck? What you need to be thinking about is the fact that Karen has gotten away, with her son Oscar. Because although Bambi's crew got most of the Klan, with them on the loose, they might as well have gotten nobody. If anything, that may come back on us."

"Come back on us how?" Carissa asked. "NIGGA tore down Emerald City and Camelot. We don't have no money, because the one hundred thousand I took into the compound mysteriously got away with Karen and her son. And, since the Feds are not involved, we still don't know who stole our millions from the overseas accounts. Even though, and I'll keep most of this to myself, I think Mercedes may be involved. Not only that, we living on somebody else's grace right now. So please tell me, Thickums, what else do we have that Karen and her son could possibly want? The air coming out of our stanking asses?"

"You think we gonna stay down forever?" Yvette asked. "Bitch, I'm just getting started. You can if you want to, but I'm not gonna take this broke shit lying down. I'm a queen, and a queen sits on her thrown, not bow down too it. If you gonna give thought to anything, give thought to that." Yvette stormed off and left Carissa alone.

"You have your thoughts, Yvette, and I'll have mine," Carissa said to herself, as she continued to eye Mercedes with malice tinted shades.

PITBULLS

IN A

SKIRT 5

THE FALL FROM GRACE

CARTEL PUBLICATIONS
PRESENTS
They never wanted the power,
but they stepped to the throne
PRETTY
KINGS
T. STYLES
NATIONAL BEST SELLING AUTHOR OF *RAUNCHY*

Drunk
& Hot Girls
THE COMPLETE SERIES
By
LEGACY CARTER

THE CARTEL PUBLICATIONS

"We Reign Supreme"